"Why did you come back?"

"Because there's something unfinished."

"Don't be silly." The words were as cutting and scornful as she could make them. "What we had was a one-night stand. It was good, but that was all it was. The very essence of a one-night stand is that nothing is expected, no commitment—"

"If it was simply a one-night stand, why are you so angry with me, and why am I back here?"

She began to say that she didn't want him there, then fell silent.

"Why are you afraid?"

Before she had time to react, his hands fastened on to her shoulders. Blair stared up into an implacable face, its harsh contours lovingly delineated by the moonlight. "No," she said, but her voice was a whisper.

"Yes, you beautiful liar."

ROBYN DONALD has always lived in Northland in New Zealand, initially on her father's stud dairy farm at Warkworth, then in the Bay of Islands, where she lives today with her husband and one Corgi dog. She resigned from her teaching position when she found she enjoyed writing romances more, and now spends her spare time reading, gardening, traveling and writing letters to keep up with her two adult children and her friends.

Books by Robyn Donald

HARLEQUIN PRESENTS PLUS

1639—PAGAN SURRENDER

HARLEQUIN PRESENTS

1464—SOME KIND OF MADNESS
1505—STORM OVER PARADISE
1537—THE GOLDEN MASK
1565—ONCE BITTEN, TWICE SHY
1577—THE STONE PRINCESS
1611—SUCH DARK MAGIC

ROBYN DONALD

Paradise Lost

Harlequin Books

TORONTO • NEW YORK • LONDON
AMSTERDAM • PARIS • SYDNEY • HAMBURG
STOCKHOLM • ATHENS • TOKYO • MILAN
MADRID • WARSAW • BUDAPEST • AUCKLAND

ISBN 0-373-11666-7

PARADISE LOST

This edition published by arrangement with Harlequin Enterprises B. V.

Printed in U.S.A.

CHAPTER ONE

COLOUR deepened along Blair Doyle's cheekbones, a soft apricot not summoned by the heat, although the air was humid and warm. A year on Fala'isi had acclimatised her to the tropics. Nor was it caused by the admiring group of men who surrounded her, although they were handsome enough, and extremely attentive. A sports team on their way back to New Zealand from a tournament in Europe, they were holidaying on the island for a week. Those who were attached had had their wives and girlfriends flown in from New Zealand; almost all the others were clustered around Blair.

'More champagne, Miss Doyle?' The waiter hovered, white teeth flashing in his golden Polynesian face as he gave her a conspiratorial smile.

Wry amusement twinkled in Blair's pale green eyes. 'No, thanks, Rata, but I'd love a lime and soda,' she said quietly.

'I'll get you one.'

Now the skin on the back of her neck was being pulled tight in an irresistible, ancient response. Both the hot cheeks and the prickly sensation meant that someone was watching her.

The group around her broke into laughter as one of the men finished a story against himself. Blair had to force a smile. They were doing their best to entertain her, to make an impression. It wasn't their fault they weren't succeeding, and she had manners enough to hide her boredom. Besides, she'd have accepted Sam Vaile's invitation to the party if it had meant turning out in a hurricane. Tonight was one night she didn't want to be alone.

The notice of her final decree absolute had arrived in the mail that day, along with a letter from Penny Harding, an erstwhile friend in New Zealand, who wished her a happy thirtieth birthday, yet in the next paragraph informed her with barely concealed relish that Gerald Cartwright, who had once been Blair's husband, and his new young girlfriend had just had a baby son.

Although Blair no longer loved Gerald, his betrayal still left a bitter taste in her mouth. That he had a child when he'd spent the five years of their marriage telling her that he really didn't want a family so soon only increased her anger and resentment.

Which was no excuse for drinking one glass too many of champagne, of course. Accepting the lime juice with a warm smile, she turned her attention back to the men around her.

'So you live here permanently,' one of them said, a note of envy in his voice as he looked over the terrace towards the lagoon glittering beneath the stars. 'Lucky you! I thought it was pretty near impossible to get residence on Fala'isi.'

'It is. They're very fussy about who gets to live here, understandably. I'm here on a sort of scholarship.'

They looked impressed, almost disbelieving. One, slightly younger than the rest and more brash, even said, 'You don't look the academic type.' *Too pretty*, his tone and the look that accompanied his words indicated.

Blair grinned. 'I've met some stunning academic types in my time,' she returned drily, 'both male and female, but you're right, I'm not. I'm an artist.' And, forestalling the inevitable question, 'I paint landscapes. One caught the eye of the Prime Minister at an exhibition in Auckland and he suggested I come here and spend a couple of years painting the island. So here I am.'

'Getting inspiration,' an older man said, nodding knowledgeably.

The brash one looked at her with a sudden unpleasantly speculative gleam, no doubt wondering whether she was as bohemian in her habits as artists were supposed to be. Blair parried his stare with coolly dismissive composure. Weariness crept through her. Her admirers were pleasant and amusing and openly appreciative of her fair good looks, but they seemed so very young.

The party had turned stale. She should have stayed at home where she could grieve in decent solitude, instead of trying to find relief in company. In the last two and a half years she had learned that if she tried to hide from her pain it went underground and ambushed her when she least expected it.

For another ten minutes she made them laugh, dazzling them effortlessly. It was easy to do; her greatest friend had said often enough and enviously that Blair had a positively indecent amount of charm. It wasn't much use when it came to the important things of life, like growing older and being divorced, but it certainly helped smooth ordinary social intercourse.

Eventually she extricated herself with a quip that set them all laughing again, and strolled across the crowded room towards her host, Sam Vaile, who managed the resort.

He was talking to a man she hadn't seen before. A new guest, she concluded after a swift, startled glance at the newcomer. Certainly he didn't look like a member of the sports team. And she was prepared to wager that he was the man whose eyes had caused that swiftly primitive response.

Lean, austerely handsome, he gave Blair an overwhelming impression of intense emotions subdued by a fierce, unrelenting will. The stark black and white of his dinner-jacket contrasted with auburn highlights in his hair and threw into strong relief a face carved by time and self-discipline into a striking copper mask.

He was, Blair realised with an odd little lurch in her stomach, the most handsome creature she had ever seen, but there was not a sign of warmth in those angular features or the clear, brilliant blue eyes that watched her so dispassionately as she moved towards him.

And he was tall! Blair was almost six feet, but this man had a good three inches on her. Yet for all his height and breadth of shoulder and chest he was not like some of the athletes in the group behind her, muscled so heavily that they looked uncomfortable, almost ponderous.

This man stood unmoving, with the poised, alert stance of a sleek and powerful predator, at once aloof and watchful, in the scene yet not part of it.

'Ah, Blair,' Sam, a pleasant, intelligent Australian said enthusiastically, 'come and let me introduce Hugh Bannatyne, a fellow countryman of yours who's going to be with us for a while. Mr Bannatyne, this is Blair Doyle.'

Clearly he was someone important, otherwise Sam would have used his first name. But it hadn't needed Sam's introduction to tell Blair that. The newcomer carried his standing for all to see in that severe countenance, its hard, straight mouth and resolute jaw and chin proclaiming an uncompromising, compelling personality, a leader.

Blair wondered how difficult it would be to transfer that face to canvas, to reproduce not only the tints and hues of his colouring, but the forcefulness and the leashed energy, the crackling aura of danger that played around him. A deep upwelling of excitement, of anticipation, lit her eyes from clear, cool green to heated jade, and she distinctly felt her fingers itch. He would make a perfect subject.

The Bannatyne man's eyes, blue as the heart of a sapphire, rested on her face, but no muscle moved in the disciplined stillness of his. He seemed to be studying her with a calculated detachment that put her immediately on her mettle. Blair was not vain, or self-important, but she had grown accustomed to masculine reaction to her tall, copper-blonde beach-girl looks.

Endeavouring to wipe every tinge of cynicism from her warm, husky voice, she said, 'Welcome to Fala'isi, Mr Bannatyne.'

His hand was hard and firm, without calluses, so he didn't do hard physical labour, and he judged his grip nicely, making sure he didn't crush her fingers. Yet Blair had to fight to keep the smile on her face, to stop the sudden involuntary tightening of the muscles in her throat. That physical magnetism, the subtle yet compelling charisma that indicated a potent, forceful masculinity, found its way through her defences with alarming ease.

But what impinged most vividly was Hugh Bannatyne's studied self-control. This was not a man who allowed himself to be easily impressed. Blair sensed that his emotions had always been strongly curbed by his will. However, something had honed that in-built restraint until it was as much a part of his character as the blazing, white-hot sexuality that kept every woman in the room sliding him swift sideways glances.

Blair drew her hand away, aware of the first flickerings of awareness, of the sweet, perfidious attraction she had learned to resist.

The mark of her wedding-ring had long been burned away by the tropical sun of Fala'isi, but for a moment she thought those amazingly blue eyes might have been able to see some traces of it.

'Ms Doyle.' He had a beautiful voice, deep, yet collected and impersonal. 'How do you do?'

Again, not the reaction she was used to getting. You've become spoilt, she thought, irony creeping into the smile she kept resolutely pinned to her wide mouth. Perhaps this is what happens to divorced women of thirty. Their looks fade and men no longer watch them with any sort of interest.

'How do you do? Are you here for long?' she asked politely, flexing the hand by her side with the eerie sensation of having been branded, not on her skin but in her soul.

Broad shoulders moved a fraction, as though he had started a shrug then decided against it. 'Ten days or so,' he said.

Clearly a man of few words. Blair gave him her most entrancing smile, said earnestly, 'I do hope you enjoy your stay. Perhaps I'll see you around the island some time,' and turned to Sam. 'I must go now,' she said, real affection softening the surface glitter of her smile. 'Thanks for inviting me; it's been a super party. Your sportsmen are a charming lot.'

'Hey, I'm an Australian, remember? A follower of Aussie Rules, to boot, which is a man's game. *You're* the Kiwi.' Grinning, he bent to kiss her cheek. Sam was in the throes of a divorce too, which gave them some sort of fellow-feeling. He was demonstrative, but did not expect anyone to take his kisses or hugs the wrong way.

'Goodnight.' Blair's smile altered a fraction as her eyes met those of the man who stood beside Sam, courteously inclining his head.

The light caught Hugh Bannatyne's hair, sparking a darkly rufous shimmer in the smooth waves. His expression was stern, completely detached, but the unmistakable physical impact sent a sudden shiver down Blair's spine.

It had to be an unwanted reaction to his unleashed maleness, just a swift, sensual tug at her equilibrium, and she was not, she thought as she moved through the crowded room, going to respond to it in any but the most basic way. After all, he showed no such interest in her.

Her lips tucked down at the corners in self-derision. She didn't need an easy, quick response from Hugh Bannatyne or any other man to feed her ego!

Unfortunately for her intentions, the island band struck up a gay, totally irresistible tune, and began to sing.

Blair continued purposefully towards the doors, but before she had gone more than two steps a voice she recognised as the young man who had implied she looked too pretty to be an academic commanded, 'Dance with me, Blair.'

Her first instinct was to refuse, but the good manners her mother had drummed into her persuaded her into agreeing. Hoping that he wouldn't see her unwillingness, she ignored the significant smile he gave her and went with him on to the dance-floor.

An hour later, hot and tired and cross, Blair decided that her mother had a lot to answer for. Politeness was all very well, but she really hadn't wanted to dance. Now her skirt was clammy about her waist and long legs, and her hair stuck unpleasantly to her temples and across the back of her neck.

Perhaps she should get it cut, she thought acidly as she disentangled herself from her latest partner and waited her opportunity to slide inconspicuously away. Thirty was probably too old to be wearing hair down to one's shoulder-blades!

Her green eyes drifted around the noisy room. Sam was working the crowd, but his companion, the Bannatyne man, had gone.

Good job, too. He was irritatingly attractive, if you liked them patrician and cold-blooded, but she didn't need any man in her life again. Or only as a light-hearted affair, and nowadays who was silly enough to indulge in such things?

This time no one noticed her departure, and ten minutes later she was almost home, the beach curving out before her in a swath of silver. Even after a year on Fala'isi the island's beauty still had the power to stop her heart.

Sudden, painful tears filled Blair's eyes. Stopping, she lifted an elegant, long-fingered hand to wipe them away. Her mooncast shadow stretched away across the coarse coral sand, elongated yet oddly faithful to her body; there were the endless legs and wide shoulders, the narrow waist, the mane of hair giving her a definitely youthful air.

'You don't look your age,' she told her shadow, her husky voice low and passionate. 'You don't look thirty, and divorced, and alone. You don't even look cynical, and tired.'

Fala'isi was beautiful and she enjoyed living there, but her life yawned emptily ahead, without direction or purpose. Everything she had hoped for and worked towards—a husband, children, the decorating firm in Auckland—they were all gone. Hot, angry tears gathered again, threatening to spill. With a swift, furious gesture she used her handkerchief to mop them up. She would not cry. She had wept enough over Gerald. And she had made all the decisions that had brought her here to Fala'isi, even selling her half of the business to her partner Tegan Jones. Tegan Sinclair, of course, now that she was married.

Getting rid of the business had been a wrench, but it had to be done; Gerald was legally entitled to half their assets. In spite of the fact that she had supported him through his doctorate and provided both their house and their savings, he had demanded his legal settlement. Blair could have borrowed the money to keep her equity in the business, but somehow she had lost any pleasure in her work.

It had hurt to let it go. She and Tegan had built it up together, starting out young and green and eventually reaching the top; the last job she had done was New Zealand's new embassy in Zimbabwe.

In the first revulsion of feeling after Gerald's betrayal, selling up and starting again in a new occupation had seemed the best thing to do, although she sometimes wondered whether she'd been an utter coward, fleeing the wreckage of her marriage all the way from New Zealand to Fala'isi.

Behind her, music called from the resort; if she turned her head she would see the lights, and the low buildings, none taller than the palms they were nestled among. If she needed to reassure herself that she was still woman enough to attract a man, all she had to do was go back and she could flirt and laugh, even go to bed with one of the sportsmen if she wanted to.

The idea filled her with nausea.

Setting her chin, she made her way towards the house she was living in, a tropical fantasy built by an American who found time to visit it once every three years or so. Blair was house-sitting, although why she was needed she really didn't know. Crime seemed to be practically non-existent on Fala'isi.

There were no other houses on the beach, and the hotel guests rarely wandered down this end, so she was startled when a patch of darkness under the rustling coconut palms turned out to be more solid than the rest, and a deep voice bade her, 'Good evening.'

A New Zealander, she noted automatically, although the typical drawl had been modified by a clipped, autocratic intonation. Of course. Hugh Bannatyne.

'Good evening,' she replied warily. Fala'isi might be as safe as anywhere could be in this world, but there had been the occasional incident. She gave him a perfunctory smile and walked past rapidly.

Had he heard her impassioned remarks to her shadow? Heat prickled uncomfortably beneath her skin, but she gave a mental shrug. If he had, who cared? She wasn't likely to see him again. It was just embarrassment that made her skin crawl.

But after her shower, when she had pulled her thin, coral and white striped seersucker dressing-gown around her, instead of going to bed Blair wandered off into the air-conditioned room she used as a studio and sat down to sketch with sure strokes the face of the man who had watched her come down the beach. There had been something predatory in that silent scrutiny, something primally intent.

When she finished the sketch a self-mocking smile curved her mouth. She had captured the strong, severe cast of his features, and the way the powerful moulding of his mouth hinted at sensuality yet indicated a masculine threat the strict control couldn't quite hide. A small shiver edged icily across her skin.

Dracula? Wish-fulfilment? Every woman's secret fantasy, the dark, demon lover, the dangerous, irresistible male? Even if Hugh Bannatyne was interested in her, as instinct warned he was, she'd be an idiot to have anything to do with him. A centimetre above the paper her forefinger traced the ruthless contours of his face: straight noise, determined chin, that sculpted, ambiguous mouth. What had made him so determined not to let anyone through the barricades of his control?

Banishing the man, and the day, from her mind, she went to bed. After a while she even slept, to wake to one of the fresh, tender tropical mornings that made Fala'isi so delightful. As she lay in the huge double bed listening to the intermittent, evocative coo of a dove in the breadfruit tree, Blair decided that she'd passed a milestone.

Now that it was over, the divorce through, her birthday gone, she could stop mourning and get on with the rest of her life.

After breakfast she put some of her work—the bright, cheerful acrylics of the island that sold so well—into a carrier and walked along the sand towards the hotel. It was already hot, but as yet both the beach and the water were deserted. The tourists who stayed at the resort tended to breakfast late, not emerging until the sun was high and scorching in the sky, thereby, as far as Blair was concerned, missing the best part of the day.

In the foyer she headed towards the gift shop, but was stopped halfway across by Sam.

'New pictures?' he asked. 'Good, Asa's really pleased with the way yours are selling. The tourists who know quality when they see it just love your stuff.'

Her slow smile lit up her face. Sam was a nice man. 'Bless them. Between them all they keep the wolf very satisfactorily from the door.'

He grinned, and leered, patting her backside. 'How about opening the door for this wolf?'

Blair laughed, a lazily sensual sound in the cool, airy foyer, and opened her eyes wide, batting her lashes at him. 'Sorry, but you're an Australian. No decent New Zealand girl would sully her love-life with an Australian.'

Although Sam pretended to be a lady's man, whatever emotional depth he had was expended on his children, who flew in from Australia during the holidays, so Blair felt quite safe with the mock flirtation.

He groaned. 'How dare you insult my country like that? I'll have to—— Uh-oh, there's Hugh Bannatyne. He wants to see me. We'll continue this interesting discussion later, my dear!'

Without looking towards the Bannatyne man, Blair walked across the smooth ceramic tiles towards the gift shop, where she was greeted with enthusiasm by the proprietor, and led into the small cubbyhole behind a beaded curtain at the back of the shop.

'Good,' Asa said. 'Now, let me see them.'

Five minutes later Blair felt a peculiar tension in her scalp, and looked up, to realise that while she and Asa had been talking Hugh Bannatyne had walked silently into the shop.

Recognition was instant. He dominated the space, became its focal point, effortlessly drawing the eye with his unstudied male magnetism. Unlike most tourists he wasn't looking around the stock; he was standing with that waiting, watchful, unnerving patience, his brilliant gaze fixed on the beaded curtain.

Nodding towards the doorway, Blair nudged Asa.

Immediately the shop manager went out, her lovely smile even more spontaneous than normal. As well it might be, Blair thought, feeling a little winded herself. Emerging from the moon-speckled dimness beneath the palms Hugh had been a fantasy figure, but there in the confines of the shop he was breathtakingly overpowering.

'You have a couple of acrylics in your window,' he said, the ordinary words seeming to possess some strange magic because of the textured beauty of his voice. 'Have you anything else by the same artist?'

'As a matter of fact she's brought some more in today,' Asa told him, then lifted her voice. 'Blair, bring your pictures out.'

For an uneasy moment Blair stood rooted to the ground, a tide of instinctive resistance running through her. She was assailed by the sudden, baseless conviction that if she walked out through that doorway her life was never going to be the same again.

But although she had run from the shambles of her life in New Zealand she was not normally a coward. And she no longer paid any attention to intuition; hers had let her down too many times. After all, it was partly her conviction that she would be safe with him that had persuaded her to marry Gerald!

Straightening her shoulders, she lifted the selection of acrylics and brought them through, secretly glad she had chosen a pair of soft amber culottes splashed with gold and salmon and terracotta flowers to wear with her sleeveless golden T-shirt.

Hugh's startling bright eyes narrowed a second. 'Ms Doyle, good morning.' His voice was cool, the New Zealand drawl disciplined. 'I like your work, but the ones in the window are rather too pretty for my taste. Have you anything a little more complex?'

'Look through those,' Asa said, indicating the acrylics. 'If you can't find anything to suit you, Blair can show you some of her other works. The ones she sells here are for a particular audience, you understand.'

'Of course. Tourists.' Dark, straight brows drawn together, he began to leaf through the pile.

Blair had to drag her eyes away from his face. Portraiture was not her strong point, but she longed to take up the challenge of that striking face with its disconcerting mixture of intensity and restraint. The charcoal sketch she had done the night before hadn't satisfied her need to explore his features; only oils, she decided, would do him justice. It would be too easy to make him merely handsome, when the real interest in his face lay in the suggestion of great passion almost curbed by a will-power so stringent, so consuming, that it must take all of his energy to maintain it.

She was wondering how she would show that look of unwavering self-possession when she realised his attention was no longer on her work. He had lifted his head and was watching her with aloof detachment. Once more Blair was disconcertingly aware of heat burning along her cheekbones.

'That's an extraordinarily analytical look,' he commented quietly.

With considerable effort she managed to produce a lop-sided smile. 'It's the look that says I'd like to paint you,' she admitted.

Although his expression didn't alter she sensed the shutters falling, sealing him inside an armour of reserve, locking her out. 'I'm flattered,' he said, 'but I think not. And none of these are what I want, either. What's your other work like? More of the same?'

'No.' The word was crisp and definite.

'Blair has a studio just down the beach,' Asa volunteered when the silence threatened to become uncomfortable. Blair was one of her protégées and she was delighted to be able to help her. 'Why don't you take Mr Bannatyne down and show him some of your other work, Blair?'

Visited again by that disconcerting sense of inevitability, of foreboding, Blair said lightly, 'If you're interested, Mr Bannatyne, I can make an appointment.'

'What's wrong with now?'

Blair's head came up a fraction. 'Nothing,' she said, hoping her reluctance wasn't obvious. She did not want him anywhere near her studio or her house.

'Then I'll come down and check them out now.'

Blair said evenly, 'Oh, I can bring them up here; it's no trouble. We could use one of the small reception-rooms; the manager won't mind.'

Dark brows, straight and definite, lifted. His eyes seemed to spear through her, bluer than the ocean at midday and as translucent, yet his thoughts and responses were as concealed as his emotions.

After a moment a thin smile twisted the hard line of his mouth. 'Won't he?' he said quietly, then added with more than a touch of authority, 'I'll come with you now. You don't live far down the beach, do you?'

Before Blair could answer, Asa intervened. 'Only ten minutes or so, and it's a very pleasant walk.' She beamed at Blair, her rich smile a benediction. 'Leave those with me.'

There was nothing more to be said. Giving in gracefully, Blair said, 'Let's go, then,' and preceded Hugh Bannatyne through the door.

Blair was accustomed to attracting attention; it went with the mane of red-blonde hair and a height of almost six feet. However, now that she was accompanied by a man of such powerful male charisma, the swift, interested glances became stares.

Self-consciousness was something she believed she'd left behind with her school uniforms, but that was what seeped through her as she walked across the cool tiled floor and out into the radiant sunlight. Self-consciousness, and an inexplicable yet unavoidable conviction that she had been separated from the rest of the flock, marked out and herded to one side.

After she had shielded her eyes with her sunglasses she said politely, 'I walked down the beach, Mr Bannatyne, but if you want to drive back I can——'

'No.' He was wearing cotton trousers, as different from the normal store ones as a diamond from a piece of glass, and a fine chambray shirt. In spite of its faded colour the material emphasised the dense colour of his eyes, eyes that he covered now with sunglasses so dark that they were impenetrable. 'I'll walk down with you.'

Around them people wandered about in bright, skimpy clothes, chattering, laughing, determined to enjoy another day in paradise. The muted roar of the waves on the reef formed an ever-present counterpoint to the steady trade winds in the coconut palms. Although two of the island's brilliant blue and green and scarlet parakeets quarrelled noisily as they flew through the palms, Blair felt fancifully that she and Hugh Bannatyne were enclosed in a little cone of silence. Without speaking, they left the busy hotel behind and walked down the beach.

She had never gone this way before without trying to find some way to fit everything into a frame, the vivid colours, the freshness and the heat, the stark outlines of the mountain range that formed the core of the island, the scent of sunscreen and frangipani and coconuts and the earthy dampness of the tropics, the sea that stretched from horizon to horizon for a quarter of the way around the world, the hidden danger beneath the glamour. However, this time her whole attention was bent on the man beside her, and she resented it.

'Have you lived here long?' he surprised her by asking.

Just polite chit-chat, but she was still made uneasy by his unequivocal physical presence. 'A year,' she told him casually. 'What part of New Zealand do you come from?'

'Hawkes Bay.'

Vineyards, old money, huge homesteads and a superb climate... He looked as though he belonged there.

He continued, 'Where did you live before you came here?'

'Auckland.' She could be as non-committal as he was.

They walked on past the last of the sun-worshippers, out of sight of the sideways glances and the ripple of interest that had been voiceless but obtrusive. Neither spoke, and to Blair's sensitised nerves the distance seemed at least half as far again as it had on the way up to the hotel.

A hundred metres from the house a small canoe with a tattered woven sail had been drawn up on the beach.

'Good morning,' Blair said, smiling at the two young men who waited for her. She was one of their regular customers. 'What have you got for me today?'

Grinning, they produced a tuna, sleek as a torpedo. When she took out her purse the older of the youths said diffidently, 'My mother says will you paint a picture for her, and we will give you fish until it is paid for?'

He kept his eyes fixed respectfully downwards. On Fala'isi, as in all Polynesian societies, it was not considered polite to look into the the eyes of those who were older, or had more prestige.

'Yes, of course.' Blair hoped her voice wasn't as puzzled as she was. 'What sort of picture?'

Producing a scuffed photograph from his pocket, he held it out. 'It is my mother's brother,' he explained. 'He died in Australia and this is his headstone. My mother has told you this, but she did not tell you she wants a picture of it for the house.'

Understanding immediately, Blair nodded. 'Yes, I can do that. How big does she want it?'

He showed her, about twenty inches by twenty, and then, solemnities over, beamed at her. 'She sent you this coconut,' he said cheerfully, and handed over a green one, adding with a mischievous grin, 'Put it in the fridge and it will make a good drink for you and your man this afternoon.'

Blair's smile remained steady, but it took an effort of will. Ignoring Hugh Bannatyne's intimidating presence beside her, she said, 'Thank you,' and waved as the two boys pushed the little craft into the water and set off across the lagoon.

'Do you do much of that sort of work?' he asked.

Did that mocking undertone to the words indicate he thought she was a rank amateur? Well, he would soon find out.

A note of reserve cooled her voice. 'This is the first time. Their mother is a housemaid at the hotel, a widow, and her brother used to send her money. It's thanks to him that the boys went through high school instead of having to leave. I didn't realise she was steeling her courage to ask me to do this, but I don't mind. It's the only remembrance she's likely to have of her brother's grave.'

'I see.' He sounded almost amused.

Blair flashed him an indignant glance, but was balked by the total lack of expression in his face. If the prospect of her painting from a photograph did amuse him, there were no signs of it. 'Here we are,' she said shortly.

Her temporary home was set in a lawn of coarse grass, flagrantly green, that finished in a stone balustrade above the sand. Both house and balustrade had been built of coral by local workers, and in spite of their formal, classical incongruity managed to look at home on this Polynesian shore. A path of crushed shells led through a palm grove, past flamboyant hibiscus bushes and fragrant, sensual drifts of frangipani, to the wide terrace.

'Come in,' Blair said, that disturbing presentiment of danger making her voice oddly stiff, without resonance. 'I'll just put the fish and the coconut in the fridge.'

'Where is your studio? I can look at your work while you're attending to your domestic details.'

'It's inside,' she said briefly, stung by what seemed to be condescension in his tone. 'Through here.'

As she said the words she froze. Had she put away the sketchpad she'd been doodling on last night? It was too late to worry about it now, but she sighed with relief when a harried glance around the studio revealed that the pad was safely hidden.

'The ones for sale are along there,' she said, indicating the rows of stacked canvases along one side of the wall. She bent to pick one up, and found it taken from her hands.

'I'll look,' he said firmly.

She nodded, understanding. Nothing annoyed her more than to have someone hovering over her when she was trying to make a decision. 'I'll make us a drink,' she said awkwardly.

He looked up at her. An unexpected and wholly tantalising smile curved the hard mouth, gleamed in the sapphire eyes. 'Not coconut milk, I hope?'

Blair grinned. 'No,' she agreed, conscious of a sudden shift in her attitude. When he wasn't being a stuffed shirt he was attractive. Hazardously so.

But his smile died immediately, to be replace by that guarded watchfulness. 'I don't think I want a drink, thank you.' His voice was even and uninflected, dismissive. Without taking any further notice of her he began to look through her canvases.

Suit yourself, she thought, obscurely hurt. Aloud she said, 'Let me know if I can help,' and left him to it.

Twenty minutes later he came out. Looking up from the long cane sofa where she was pretending to read a magazine, Blair asked, 'Did you find anything you liked?'

'Yes, three oils.'

She uncurled and slid her feet into tan sandals before standing up. 'I—oh, good.' As a response it sounded lame even to her ears.

Standing back to let her go ahead of him, he observed, 'You don't sound madly elated to have sold three canvases. I assume you have no difficulty getting rid of your work.'

Blair didn't want to tell him anything about herself but politeness insisted on a response. 'The acrylics of the island sell like hot cakes.' To her irritation the words came out with a slight defensive intonation.

'I can understand why. They're not ordinary tourist fare. There's more than a hint of passion beneath the excellent technique, and certainly intelligence there.'

She sent him a quick, startled look. 'Thank you,' she said after a moment's hesitation. 'I gather you're something of a connoisseur?'

The wide shoulders moved in a shrug. 'I know what I like,' he returned, a sardonic smile not softening his mouth.

Blair took the implication. 'But I'll bet you know more than a little about art.'

'Enough to know that you're wasting your time producing pretty views to remind tourists of their South Sea holiday. If you're capable of work like that stuff in there you should be doing it full-time, not whiling away your life in lotus land.'

Narrow brows lifting in something like shock, she looked away. 'I got used to eating,' she said absently, 'at a formative stage of my life, and I've never been able to convince myself that starving in a garret is preferable to doing pretty pictures now and then.'

'Why isn't a gallery interested in your work?'

'Why do I need a gallery? I could sell hundreds on Fala'isi——'

'Not here,' he interrupted calmly, those intense blue eyes fixed on her face as though he could see right through into her soul. 'Those canvases in there are not about Fala'isi, they're your response to New Zealand. You should have a gallery owner in Auckland taking every canvas he can get from you.'

Blair's smile was crooked. 'Not yet.'

He waited, but when she said nothing more he pursued, 'Why not?'

'Because in Auckland I'm known as a decorator. You know what sort of credibility that gives me?'

His straight brows shot up. 'A decorator?'

Why had she said that? She had decided to watch her tongue, and now she was giving away far too much. It was perilously easy to tell him about herself, and instinct warned her that perilous was the exact word.

'I used to decorate other people's houses. I was good at it, too,' she said coolly.

'What made you decide to give it up and come here?'

Blair shrugged, looking somewhat belligerently into his hard, disturbing face.

'I needed a change,' she said lightly, smiling, her eyes green and opaque and steady, 'and Fala'isi seemed the perfect place for it.'

'In other words, mind your own business.' His dark lashes came down to hide his thoughts.

His astuteness made her uneasy all over again. Suddenly a little ashamed of her rudeness, she said, 'I don't intend to stay here permanently, but paradise is the best place for a holiday, surely?'

'For a holiday, of course, not to live,' he asserted. 'And you don't seem to be the sort of person who accepts tourist slogans unthinkingly.'

She almost asked him what sort of person she did seem to be, and caught herself back just in time. With a tight smile she turned to see which canvases he had chosen.

They didn't surprise her; it was a tribute to the impact he'd made on her that she'd guessed correctly the ones he'd like. One was a stark, almost abstract landscape of brooding bush and river, with no human presence at all. The second was a night scene in which she had tried to avoid the easy romanticism of moon and water while conveying the inherent isolation of three small islands at the bottom of the world. New Zealand lived and breathed in both, magnificent, unfeeling, merciless. They were a product of those first months in Fala'isi when her life had seemed at an end.

Hugh Bannatyne said quietly, 'Don't you know your Tennyson? Lotus-eating leads to inertia and eventually to death, of the spirit and the soul if not the body.'

'Are you speaking from experience?'

'A life spent beachcombing has never been one of my ambitions.'

He didn't, she thought, eyeing him covertly, look like a man who had any dreams left, if he had ever had them. Some people were like that; something killed hope in them, leaving them mortally wounded. Did he find his lost dreams in art?

Bluntly, with a hint of impatience, he said, 'How much do you want for your work?'

Mortified, she bit her lip. How completely unprofessional of her not even to think of the price! Hoping her voice would not reveal her chagrin, she named a sum of money in New Zealand dollars.

'Collectively, or individually?'

Lord, he must think she was a complete fluff-brain. 'Individually,' she said too loudly.

'All right. Is the third one the same price?'

She turned the third one over. It was a scene done with meticulous attention to realistic detail, of mountains seen from the air. But these were not New Zealand mountains; there was none of the interplay of moisture and air that was so much a part of that country. These were mountains where both the land and the air had been sucked dry for milleniums, the old, old bones of mountains, fierce and cruel and malevolent. At the top of the canvas an eagle's claw slashed through the burning heat of a triangle of sky.

'That's not for sale, I'm sorry,' Blair said curtly, fighting back sudden, debilitating nausea.

'Why?'

Because it was based on an experience she still hadn't come to terms with. 'I'm sorry,' she said, her voice brittle, 'I didn't realise it was there with the other ones; it's usually kept separate.'

'If I don't get that one as well the deal's off.'

His tone was indifferent, but Blair knew a total lack of any interest in compromise when she heard it. Her hesitation was palpable; wordlessly she looked at him, reading nothing but an implacable determination in the harsh angles of his face and his unyielding gaze, blue and hard as the sky on a winter's day.

Living in Fala'isi was cheap, although she paid a share of the power costs for the house. The pretty souvenirs she painted for tourists more than covered her living expenses. But when she went back to New Zealand she would need to buy a house, and for that she needed much more money.

She looked down at the picture in her hands, seeing in it pain and terror, the raw fury and the degradation that was exposed to those with eyes to see. Hugh Bannatyne had such eyes; that he wanted to buy the work was almost a violation of her privacy.

But perhaps she should sell it to him; then she might be able to free herself of the weeks spent in El Amir. Her friend Tegan had wondered whether by keeping that series of paintings she was refusing to let go of the weeks she had spent two and a half years ago imprisoned in El Amir, a tiny Middle Eastern emirate. Possibly Tegan was right.

Blair said curtly, 'All right, you can have it.'

'How much?' His voice was completely unemotional, yet she was sure he understood something of the meaning of the works he had chosen.

A sudden flash of searing anger made her stipulate a price that should have sent him reeling back on his heels, but he said merely, 'Do you accept credit cards?'

'No.'

'I'll have to write you out a cheque, then. I'm here for a few days, so you'll be able to get it verified before I leave. I'd like a receipt.'

Cool, unhurried, businesslike. Did he have any warmth in him at all?

Blindly Blair gazed down at the painted surface until the outlines of the mountains began to blur and waver. 'Yes, of course,' she said tonelessly. 'I'll store them here until you go.'

'At least until the bank verifies the cheque,' he said blandly.

Blair wanted him out of the house. She felt that he knew too much about her, that he had seen past the defences she had erected with such care, and now knew what a wasteland her life was.

Ten minutes later she was alone, looking down at his signature, H. E. Bannatyne, written in handwriting that was decisive and forceful. No doubt a handwriting expert could tell her more about his personality than that, but it was enough for her. He frightened her in some primitive, elemental way. Her reaction owed more to instinct than to logic, and was all the more extreme because she couldn't discern the reason for it.

She decided to take the cheque into Fala'isi town immediately. A glance at her watch convinced her. The bus left the hotel in another ten or twenty minutes, depending on how many people there were on it and how far behind the schedule it was today. It was one of the island's most appealing characteristics, this refusal to be constricted by timetables, but today she hoped it wouldn't be as late as it usually was. It was stupid, and she was behaving with a total lack of rationality, but she didn't want any reminder of Hugh Bannatyne in the house at all.

The bank promised to have the cheque verified as soon as possible. Relieved, as though holding the cheque was akin to having the man near her, Blair left the building and was walking past the market in Fala'isi when she heard her name called. Reluctantly she turned. Sam Vaile was a dear, but at the moment she didn't feel like talking to anyone.

Still, she wasn't exactly good company for herself. Perhaps this was just what she needed—pleasant conversation with an interesting, charming man who set off no warning signals, no odd, inchoate presentiments.

'Hello, Blair. Did you come in on the bus? You should have let me know you wanted a lift. Lord, it's hot, isn't it? I'm exhausted, yet there you are, fresh as a daisy in spite of a temperature in the mid-thirties. How do you do it?'

She smiled. 'I walk sedately and I don't get flustered.'

Sam grinned at her. 'Whereas I run. Can I persuade you to have a cup of coffee with me at the Trader's?'

'Of course you can.'

Once inside they talked until Blair's eyes were caught by a man who walked past. Was there nowhere on the island where she would be free from Hugh Bannatyne? Dressed in immaculate lightweight wear entirely suitable for the tropics, he stood out even among the tall islanders, more because of that chilling aura of aloofness about him than for his looks, although they were striking enough. He was damnably, powerfully disturbing, with the sun striking flames from his hair and the arrogant line of his profile etched against the blue waters of the harbour.

In spite of the admiring glances he was attracting he looked essentially alone, a completely self-contained man. It struck Blair that such splendid and arrogant isolation was a warning in itself.

CHAPTER TWO

THAT was how Blair felt—cut off from the rest of humanity, an outsider. But she didn't enjoy being like that, whereas it seemed to be Hugh Bannatyne's natural state.

'An interesting man,' Sam said, just a little too casually.

Hastily recalled to her surroundings, Blair nodded. 'Yes. He bought three of my paintings an hour ago.'

Sam looked a little taken aback, then openly pleased. 'Did he? Good for you! He's a bit of an enigma, the same guy. He must be loaded, though; he's staying in the Ambassador's Suite. Usually he stays with the Chapmans.'

On the surface this meant nothing, but Grant Chapman was a powerful man. His family had been on the island for as long as Europeans had been in the South Pacific—the original Chapman had married the daughter of the last paramount chief. Their descendants had used the island as a base to build up a sphere of influence that extended all around the Pacific. On the island they possessed as much prestige as the high chief. The Prime Minister had consulted Grant Chapman before he'd signed Blair's permit to stay on Fala'isi.

She knew them; she had been to dinner several times at their palatial house, and they had accepted her reciprocal invitations with every appearance of enjoyment. Tamsyn Chapman was a New Zealander, which had made a bond, but they lived lives that were vastly different from Blair's. If Hugh Bannatyne was a friend of theirs then he was someone of considerable importance.

'So why isn't he staying with them this time?' Blair asked.

Sam shrugged. 'They're in England, and the house is being cleaned and painted from top to toe. But when I got a note from head office telling me to extend all help etc., etc., to Mr Bannatyne, I detected the Chapman hand. What did you think of Hugh Bannatyne?'

'Very—self-sufficient.'

'Isn't he just!' Sam bestowed a smile on a couple weighed down with souvenirs who immediately stopped to tell him how much they were enjoying their stay. He dealt with them courteously, his professional charm very much to the fore.

When at last they left he said, 'I wish I had whatever it is that Bannatyne's got. He only has to sit down for a minute and women start drifting his way. He's perfectly polite, but so far they've all gone off disappointed. I overheard one tell a friend that it was a pity to waste a face and body like that on someone who wasn't a man, more a force of nature, like an iceberg or a glacier.'

In his own way Sam was quite good-looking; his regular features and open, smiling expression probably made him more conventionally handsome than Hugh Bannatyne. What Sam didn't have was the electrifying intensity, the assured, dynamic masculinity that clung about Hugh like an aura.

'And he seems to enjoy being by himself,' Sam went on. 'You know, you see the other loners—most of them would love to tie up with someone else so they have company, but he's happy on his own. In fact, happier like that. As you say, self-contained.'

'I'm all for self-containment,' Blair replied easily. Hugh had disappeared, but she still felt icy little sensations trickle down her spine.

Sam looked at her. 'You've got it too, that air of—oh, composure, inner certainty, I suppose you could call it. Not quite like Bannatyne, though. You're not as hard-edged as he is.'

'I hope not.' Blair drank more coffee, trying to think of some way to steer the conversation away from Hugh.

'Still, I suppose if you're an international lawyer you have to be tough,' Sam said.

'What on earth is an international lawyer?'

He grinned. 'I've only got a sketchy idea, but that's what Hugh Bannatyne is.'

'How do you know that?'

'Someone in the bar last night had come across him professionally. Apparently he works with international companies who have interests in New Zealand. The guy I was talking to said he has such a reputation for brilliance he can pick and choose his clients. If you're a multi-national company and you want to do a deal with someone in the South Pacific, you try to persuade Hugh Bannatyne to work for you. He's old money, apparently, which would give him all the contacts he needs. The chap at the bar last night said he was noted for his honesty and fairness, but he's tougher than a gimlet gum. According to him, more than a few companies have retired licking their wounds after he'd finished with them.'

Such a background and such a reputation would certainly explain Hugh's arrogant self-confidence, and the aristocratic air that grated Blair's nerves. Made uncomfortable by her own interest in the man, an interest that was veering dangerously close to fascination, she finished her coffee and coaxed Sam to tell her what had happened a couple of days before when a famous film star and his supposed niece had been surprised by his wife in their hideaway on the other side of the island.

Sam told a good story, and almost immediately she forgot Hugh Bannatyne. 'How do you know all this?' she gasped when he'd finished, trying to stifle her laughter.

'The same way everyone on the island knows everything,' he said, pleased with her response. 'The house-girl there is a cousin to old Pere Upulu, who is Philip Motiti's father-in-law.'

Blair primmed her mouth. 'And is it a part of Philip's duties as your second-in-command at the Coral Sands to fill you in on all the gossip?'

'Of course. Young Sina, your housegirl, is Philip's cousin, so it's a wonder she didn't tell you all about it.'

'We don't see much of each other, really. I'm busy when she comes in, and that's only three days a week. I see more of her husband when he mows the lawn.'

'Well, I suppose I shouldn't be gossiping,' Sam said a little guiltily, 'and I wouldn't, only the bastard skipped off leaving us quite a bill in the bar.'

'That doesn't sound like your bar staff. I'd have thought they were far too alert to be caught like that.'

'It was a new chap, innocent and fresh from the wilds of New Zealand, and still somewhat awed by it all, especially film stars with easy manners and world-famous faces and ravishing red-headed "nieces". He won't make that mistake again. Are you ready to go? I don't want to hurry you away, but I have an appointment shortly.'

'If I'm going to catch the bus I'd better get moving, I suppose.' Blair got to her feet and picked up her bag.

Out in the street she perched her sunglasses on her nose, screwing up her eyes momentarily at the contrast between the shade under the wide verandas and the dancing, dazzling sunlight in the middle of the road.

'I'll be off,' Sam said, dropping a friendly kiss on her cheek. 'Do you want a ride home? If you do, be at the car park at four.'

'No, thanks, I'll catch the three o'clock bus back.'

He looked at his watch. 'You're running late, then. It leaves in five minutes.'

'Come on, Sam, when have you ever known it to be on time?'

'True. Actually, you'll probably get home faster if you wait for me,' he pointed out, grinning.

Blair laughed up at him, but said, 'I like travelling in the bus. Thank you for the drink—see you later.'

After crossing the busy street she had taken only a few steps towards the bus station when she saw Hugh Bannatyne standing in the discreetly opulent entrance of a shop ahead, talking to a man she recognised as the manager. Her eyes flicked from his starkly etched profile to the shop windows.

So he had been looking at pearls, the exquisite black and gold pearls for which Fala'isi was famous. And judging by the fact that Piripi Ovalau, looking inordinately satisfied, had escorted him to the doorway, he hadn't come away empty-handed.

Must be nice to be some people. Those pearls cost more than a guilt-free conscience. Who was he buying them for? A wife? He was about thirty-five, thirty-six, which meant there should be a wife tucked away somewhere. But he didn't look married, somehow. He looked—well, *solitary*. Not lonely, just completely and entirely alone.

Carefully and deliberately keeping her distance, Blair walked along behind him, even reducing her speed when his pace slowed. It was stupid, and again she was behaving irrationally, but she didn't want to catch up with him.

However, he must have sensed her presence, for after a hundred yards or so he looked over his shoulder. Of course Blair's gaze happened just then to be directed his way. For a moment she thought that he was going to stare straight through her, but even as she composed her face for rejection he smiled.

It was not a pleasant smile. Contempt was there, and a cold scorn. He thinks I'm following him, she thought disconnectedly. He nodded, and then quite deliberately swung across the street.

It was like a slap in the face. Humiliation roiled through her in hateful waves; her steps faltered, and for a horrible moment tears stung her eyes.

Sheer pride brought her head up, cast her features into stiff rigidity. How dared he? If he assumed that every woman who walked behind him was following him he had a damned good opinion of himself. Stuffy, haughty bastard! Blair set off for the bus station, the heels of her sandals clicking angrily on the hot concrete footpath.

She arrived to find the bus not there yet, and had to wait. After half an hour of pleasant chat seated in the shade of a raintree, she said to the woman beside her, 'The bus is later than it usually is, isn't it?'

'Where are you going?'

'To the Coral Sands resort.'

The woman looked surprised. 'That bus has gone.'

Sure enough, the one occasion that Blair had arrived late, the bus had left on time. Sighing, she consulted her watch. She could go back into town and wait for Sam, but if she set off walking home Sam had to go past her, and would stop and pick her up. Although it was hot she was accustomed to it by now. Like the islanders, she would just take her time. Grasping her bag, she set off.

Twenty minutes later she was walking down an avenue of magnificent frangipani bushes, bathed in their scent and trying to work out the exact shade of their blossoms, a subtle blending of maroon and dark crimson, and how she would convey it to her canvas. A pang of home-sickness almost overwhelmed her; each year she and Tegan used to picnic in the Parnell Rose Gardens in Auckland, and they'd go around and smell each of the roses, losing themselves in the perfume, while she decided how she would reproduce the precise colour and form of each one.

Good practice, she thought now, for making a living with a paintbrush. It was then that a car drew up behind her.

Smiling, she turned. Unfortunately the man who looked out through the car window was not Sam. Her heart gave a frantic skip in her throat. Jamming her sunglasses back on to her nose, she met Hugh Bannatyne's enigmatic gaze. 'Hello,' she said inanely, trying not to feel as though she had just been dunked in icy seas without a chance to catch her breath.

He wound down the window and asked with aloof courtesy, 'Can I give you a ride back?'

She shook her head, trying to be sensible and matter-of-fact. 'I'm waiting for Sam Vaile to come along,' she said.

His brows rose but he didn't take his eyes from her face. 'You're going to be waiting quite some time. I saw him in the bar of the Trade Winds, and it didn't look as if he planned to leave in a hurry,' he said drily. 'You'd better get in.'

Blair was going to refuse, she knew she was, yet no words left her mouth, and instead of shaking her head she nodded. Just like an adolescent, she thought, fuming as his mouth curled in that cold, unamused smile, her instant realisation that she had made the wrong decision intensified by the mockery which flickered in the gentian-blue eyes for an instant.

But what harm could that do, just driving back with him? She was over-reacting, of course. She used to be so confident around men, manoeuvring them with her lazy smile and a flash of smoky green eyes between dark lashes; since El Amir she monitored every thought, every gesture, in case it should deliver the wrong message.

She hated being like this, held prisoner by a threat that no longer existed. But although she had gone to a therapist nothing seemed to have have helped. She had been unable to respond to any man, even Gerald. In the end, when Gerald had left her for a younger, untraumatised woman, she had cut her losses and run away to paradise.

And she was happy here. In spite of Hugh Bannatyne's unconcealed scorn for lotus-eating, she revelled in island life. Freed for the first time in her adult life from responsibilities, she had given herself to painting, discovering in the process that what she had at first thought to be a hobby had become an overwhelming compulsion. She was not vainglorious—she knew she would never be in the top ranks of artists—but she accepted that almost gratefully. David Andrews, the only important painter she knew, was driven by his art, unable to exist without it, so powerfully obsessed that it left him no energy for anything else. Blair almost pitied him, for it seemed to her that he had sacrificed everything—his marriage, his children, contentment and peace—to the voracious demands of his muse. Blair didn't think she had the will-power to follow her star so single-mindedly. She was content to produce her best work and draw what mental and emotional sustenance she could from her efforts, but she needed friends and affection to make her life complete.

A small, totally cynical smile flicked up the corners of her wide, soft mouth. Perhaps she should try to become as driven and dedicated as David; unless she was able to overcome the disabling memories of her imprisonment in El Amir, she was not going to find love or affection with any man ever again. Although it was hard to forgive Gerald his betrayal, she was forced to admit that he had considered his reasons unassailable. Men, he had told her, needed the physical expression of love far more than women.

He was probably right. Blair had to admit that she'd never felt anything like the ecstasies novels promised. Making love had been a pleasant experience, she had enjoyed it, but the experience had always left her wondering what all the fuss was about. After a while she had decided that possibly she just wasn't a very sensual woman.

Unfortunately her violent physical reaction to the man who was opening the door for her now seemed to indicate that she might have been wrong.

Her pale eyes darkened. As the car door closed firmly on her, she decided that until they got back to the hotel she would be very calm, very restrained, very poised. The memory of that look Hugh had given when he thought she was following him, and the arrogance with which he had got rid of her, ate into her composure like acid, but she was going to show him that he needn't worry. He might do strange things to her nerves, but she wasn't in the least interested in any relationship. Men were more trouble than they were worth.

After he'd set the vehicle in motion he asked, 'Do you mind if I turn the air-conditioning off and wind the windows down? Once the car's cool I prefer not to use the air-conditioning.'

'I don't mind in the least. I always do that, too. I know good Greenies would probably think it was being hypocritical, but I convince myself every little bit does help to save the ozone layer.' As the windows slid down, Blair took a black bandeau from her bag and slipped it over her head, anchoring the flying tresses back from her face.

'That is amazing hair,' he observed. 'Like living, growing sunlight, a mixture of copper and gold.'

He spoke without emphasis, yet Blair sent him an uneasy look, and was rendered even more wary by the dispassionate, sideways glance that scanned her face momentarily before switching back to the road ahead.

'Thank you,' she said stiffly when the silence threatened to go on too long.

His mouth tucked in at one corner. 'Don't you like compliments? You must get them all the time. You're very beautiful.'

Once more he spoke in an oddly impersonal tone, almost as though bored by the subject. She said levelly, 'Thank you again. Or, rather, thank the genetic inheritance that gave me these fashionable features and skin colour.'

'Do you despise your looks?'

She shrugged. 'I'm not so stupid. I know they've made life easier for me in many ways, just as yours must have helped you. It's a fact of life that people respond more positively to people who look good. If they're tall too, so much the better. Still, I'd rather be complimented on my work, which takes effort and enthusiasm and sheer persistence, as well as a certain amount of skill.'

'I see.' Something in his voice made her glance up sharply, but his self-possession meant that she saw nothing beyond the slashing physical features she itched to set down on canvas. 'Your work is obviously very important to you,' he said casually.

'Yes.' Normally she didn't talk much about her work but something made her say passionately, 'It's vital, essential. I sometimes wonder how I managed to exist without it. I think I must have sublimated my need for it by decorating houses, but it was only a poor substitute at best.'

'I envy you.' It was said without inflexion, but she sensed that he was speaking the truth.

'Don't you feel that way about your profession? You're a lawyer, I believe.'

He sent her a swift, sideways look then transferred his glance back to the road. 'Yes, I am, and no, I don't feel that way about my work. I enjoy it, I'm good at it, I get considerable satisfaction from it, but I don't need it, as you obviously need yours. I could be equally satisfied by several other professions. Is your art the reason you are not married?'

It wasn't—quite—an impertinent question, but Blair bristled. Just in case he really did think she'd been following him through the streets of Fala'isi, she said crisply, 'It's certainly very difficult to have a normal relationship. Men tend to want dinner on time, and clothes washed, and baths cleaned. I enjoy my independence enormously, and I don't intend to give it up.'

'You sound very sure of that,' he said, long-fingered dark hands deft as they swung the wheel around a tight corner.

'I am,' she said firmly.

They began to climb through banana plantations, the sun refracting off the huge, shiny leaves to enclose the road in a yellow-green shadow. When she had first come to Fala'isi Blair had revelled in the unabashed fecundity, the lush, burgeoning beauty of the island, with a strange sense of coming home. The colours of the South Pacific, vibrant and overwhelming, had made her giddy, almost drunk with excitement. A year spent in surroundings of such rich, unfettered beauty hadn't dimmed her appreciation, although there were other aspects to the tropics she'd discovered she could do without.

The intense humidity, for one. Surreptitiously wiping a bead of sweat from her forehead, she darted a glance at the man behind the wheel. The sheen of moisture across his skin merely served to highlight the elemental masculinity of his features.

What was he thinking? What had happened to make him keep his emotions imprisoned so closely?

Above the banana plantations the jungle clawed up the ancient volcanoes until altitude and thinning soil prevented the growth of anything but vivid grass. Blair loved the rain forest, so exotic, so lushly beautiful. As the road began to climb steeply she looked from side to side, taking in the myriad greens, the violent juxtaposition of shape and texture. Too swiftly they reached the top of the old lava flow, swooping down the other side to more plantations, and thence into the palm forest that continued along the beach for miles, eventually leading them to the resort.

Hugh was a good driver. Without any evidence of impatience he adjusted his speed to the slow rate of progress of everything else on the road, avoiding pedestrians, chickens, and the frequent moped riders and cyclists wobbing along burdened by cargoes far too unwieldy for anything with only two wheels to cope with. His lean, competent hands responded quickly to the hazards entailed by every car journey in Fala'isi, and he acknowledged the frequent greetings from the passers-by with a smile that hinted of another, younger and more open man.

Of course he would probably, Blair acknowledged wryly, be good at anything he did, if somewhat soullessly efficient. Did he ever lose that calculated control? Perhaps when he made love...

Colour heated her already hot cheeks. As they came up to the hotel she said, 'Put me down here, I'll walk the rest of the way,' but he ignored her, driving on until they had reached the narrow white shell track that led to her house. Even then, he took her right down to the building itself.

So of course Blair had to ask him in for a drink. She made no attempt to make her tone hospitable, so she was surprised when he accepted. Something, another of those beastly premonitions, sent sharp prickles of caution through her.

She had fallen into her old habit of romanticising, trying to see through the outward armour to a man who probably didn't even exist. It had always been a dangerous thing to do, and intuition warned her that where Hugh Bannatyne was concerned it was even more so.

He carried her parcels into the house for her, and when she asked him what sort of drink he'd like said promptly, 'Long and cold, no alcohol.'

'Lime juice? There's a lime tree in the garden so the juice is fresh.'

'It sounds ideal.'

It was ideal, the perfect drink for a hot day. As she sat down opposite him on the terrace, the glass cold in her hand, Blair said gratefully, 'It's a pity mint doesn't grow here. I used to love mint and lime when I was a kid.'

'Where were you a kid?'

She had to stop her shoulders from moving restlessly. 'In Auckland,' she said, her tone dismissive. 'Are you here on business or pleasure, Mr Bannatyne?'

His straight dark brows lifted as he caught her in an uncomfortably keen gaze. 'Couldn't you call me Hugh?

Manners on the island seem almost as informal as ours are at home.'

She smiled, but didn't return the invitation. 'Only among the tourists,' she said. 'The islanders have very strict rules about protocol.' Perversely, because of course she didn't want to know anything about him, she persisted, 'Is this a holiday for you?'

'Partly, but I'm also here on business.' He drank down some more lime juice, the muscles in his tanned throat moving as he swallowed.

Deep inside Blair felt a hazardous flick of something more potent than desire. It scandalised her. To banish it she said chattily, 'You were being a bit modest when you said you were a lawyer, I think. Aren't you something very hig-powered in the legal world?'

His expression didn't alter but the crystalline eyes turned as translucent and hard as a blue diamond. 'Is Fala'isi so desperate for topics that they're reduced to talking about occasional guests?'

She laughed. 'Apparently someone recognised you at the hotel. Fala'isi is like a small village; everyone's interested in everyone else. It truly is the next best thing to paradise, I think.' Perhaps if he got nothing but platitudes from her he'd go and never come back.

The small intimations of relaxation in his body language were unmistakable. Even as Blair's heart flipped in her breast she realised that although his smile was potent and unsettling it didn't soften the austere, disciplined lines of his features at all. Amused or not, Hugh Bannatyne was in full control of his emotions.

'No place is close to paradise,' he said. 'And, if it were, humanity would ruin it very quickly. We don't understand paradise, or even happiness.'

So he was a cynic. Blair, too, had been made cynical by experience. However, she enjoyed a good discussion. Leaning forward, she took issue in as provocative a manner as she could.

Half an hour later she found herself admitting that he was brilliant, with a quick, incisive brain that tore through the ungrounded observations she was in the habit of tossing airily about. He made her think, he forced her to reason, he exhilarated her and shocked her with the speed of his responses, but she hadn't enjoyed herself so much in years.

'All right,' she said at last, half laughing, 'that's enough for today. I haven't given my brain such a workout since I came to Fala'isi.'

'Use it or lose it,' he said, getting to his feet with a lithe, unforced movement that took her by surprise.

Defensively she retorted, 'I'm not wasting my life here.'

He was too astute to let that go by unchallenged. 'It sounds as though you're trying to convince yourself.'

She shrugged, walking with him towards the door. 'Not everyone understood why I wanted to come to Fala'isi,' she acknowledged.

'And why did you?'

That was entirely too personal. However, as she opened the door Blair was horrified to hear herself saying, 'My marriage broke up. I decided to put as much distance between me and my ex-husband as possible.'

'So Fala'isi fulfilled the usual object of a tropical hideaway—it's a refuge.' His eyes swept her face, lingered on her mouth.

Blair drew in a sharp breath but refused to look away. 'At first,' she admitted, 'but I love living here now. I'm independent, I've ordered my life to suit me, I can do exactly what I want.'

'I was right, then. You're an up-market beachcomber.'

It took some effort but she managed to summon her lazily sensual smile in return, keeping her lashes lowered as she said indolently, 'Exactly. Thanks for bringing me home.'

It was a dismissal, blunt and obvious. Something untamed and dangerous sparked in the sapphire depths of his eyes, but his voice revealed nothing except a remote, edged courtesy as he replied, 'It was no trouble. Thank you for the drink, Blair. No doubt we'll see each other again.'

Not, she thought as she waved goodbye, if I see you first.

For at least ten minutes she wandered about the house, before telling herself very firmly that she had work to do. Hugh Bannatyne was an intriguing man but he wasn't part of her life, whereas earning enough to give herself a decent nest-egg when she went back to New Zealand was. She should finish the canvas she had begun the day before.

But at the door of the studio she stopped, her expression marked by a deep and driving restlessness. After a moment's hesitation she turned into her bedroom instead and got into her bathing suit, a flowered one-piece in hot, tropical colours of pink and blue and green that were a vivid contrast to her creamy peach skin. A suitable slather of sunblock over every inch of that skin and the addition of a large straw hat readied her. She slipped her feet into rubber jandals and walked across the crisp, coarse grass.

As usual, the beach outside the house was deserted, although the end down by the resort was thickly dotted with bodies—most, she was glad to see, in the shade of the big, fringed umbrellas. The days of slowly roasting oneself in the unforgiving rays of the sun seemed to be well and truly over.

After depositing her hat and jandals in the spiky shade of a coconut palm she walked into the water, silky and warm as it never was at home. Normally she loved swimming, but today the expected soothing of her spirit was lost in a turmoil of emotions.

So she was attracted to Hugh Bannatyne. She knew the signs: the instant, yet highly reluctant awareness, the slow burn of desire as it licked through her body, the hidden secret signals readying her for a man's embrace. It had happened before, but Hugh was more dangerous because he was infinitely more intelligent than the other man who had had this effect on her.

Tony Keeper, her first love, had wanted her, and enjoyed her, and used her, burning her so badly that she had decided never to surrender to the heated wildfire of passion again. Several years later she had given in to Gerald's insistence and married him, her wounded spirit craving what he offered—a dependable, gentle man who swore he loved her unreservedly. And that decision, that marriage, she thought with a painful smile, had been the biggest mistake of all.

But forewarned, as the cliché had it, was definitely forearmed, and she wasn't going to make the same mistakes again. Only idiots did that. Clearly she was unable to do whatever other women did to have a happy, mutually satisfactory relationship, so she had given up on that hope. She had learned her lesson too thoroughly. The whole circus of lust and love and attraction just wasn't for her; she didn't have the stamina for it. For companionship she would rely on friends. She had much better luck with them than she did with lovers. Her friends rarely let her down.

Rolling over on to her back, she lifted her face to the sun, peering through wet lashes that refracted the rays into tiny, brilliant rainbows. If Hugh Bannatyne wanted a holiday fling he could look elsewhere for it.

He was waiting for her when she walked up from the water, leaning against the horizontally ridged bole of the palm under which she had deposited her clothes. He looked like every woman's dream of the warrior who came in the night, the secret, forbidden lover who took without asking, giving ecstasy in return, but vanished with the dawn.

Acutely conscious that her bathing suit revealed every smooth, feminine line of her body, and that the beads of water running down her skin highlighted slender golden arms and legs, Blair pulled her hair back from her face and wound it in a knot, squeezing out the excess water. His intent, unsmiling survey, a direct intimidation, heated her flesh, setting off fires beneath the surface.

With head held high she walked swiftly across the hot white coral sand. A sudden flash of insight told her that, although he kept his emotions in continual subjection, he was as affected by her as she was affected by him. To her astonishment and chagrin, beneath the stab of sheer terror engendered by that realisation lurked a sly, wanton smugness. Angling her chin, she allowed her gaze to run over him in the same insulting, speculative way he watched her.

He had done a lot of riding; the muscle development in his legs was unmistakable. Into her wayward mind there sprang an image of him seated on a large stallion, its coal-black mane and tail flowing as they galloped across a burnt hillside. Oh, God, she thought, trying to taunt herself out of it, just what every adolescent girl yearns for!

A loose cotton shirt, patterned by an exquisite tapa design in red-browns and blacks and charcoals, showed off both the breadth of his shoulders and the strength of his arms. The designs and the shirts were produced by a group of women in the village in the next bay. They cost, Blair knew, a packet, as did the suite he was in at the hotel.

Hugh Bannatyne was very rich. Not that it was the trappings that told her so. He bore himself with the unconscious arrogance that wealth and position gave to favoured humans.

'I thought it must be you when I noticed someone swimming down here. Do you usually go so far out?' he asked, holding out her towel as she came up to him.

She shrugged it around her shoulders, not trying to hide her surprise. 'Yes. I'm competent in the water.'

'Possibly, but what if a shark came along?'

'Sharks have been known to attack in knee-deep water,' she returned drily. 'Anyway, there's never been a shark attack inside the lagoon. The islanders have this contract with them—they don't eat each other. About the only dangerous thing I'm likely to do is stand on a stonefish, and I'm very careful not to put my feet on the bottom until I reach the sand.

His smile was ironic. 'So I'm fussing.'

'It's kind of you, but yes, you are fussing. Actually, I think the hotel would probably notice if anything went wrong and one of the runabouts would be over fairly quickly.'

'Are you and the manager lovers?'

For a moment she didn't believe she had heard correctly. A quick, stunned glance at his face convinced her she had; he was watching her with cool detachment, as though he had no emotional involvement in the answer, or the impulse that prompted the question. Judging by his demeanour he was merely seeking information.

Anger lit a slow fuse inside her. When she finally responded it was with crisp, icy composure. 'It is none of your business, but no, we are not lovers.' And in case this was the forerunner to a proposition she finished frostily, 'I am not looking for a lover.'

'I don't know that I asked that,' he said, mockery gleaming in the blue depths of his eyes.

Blair gave him the look which had daunted more people than she could count, picked up her jandals and her hat, then walked straight past him.

'You forgot your watch.' His voice was smooth as cream, with an infuriating note of amusement running like a hidden river through it.

Biting her lip, Blair hastily composed her face into blandness then swung around, holding out an imperative hand. Instead of dropping the watch into her palm he fastened the slim leather band around her wrist. The touch of his fingers, light but positive, seared like tracks of fire across her skin. Blair's heart began to beat heavily in her ears. Beads of sweat popped out across her top lip, at her temples. She took a swift involuntary step backwards and said unevenly, 'Thank you,' before turning away.

Good manners or not, she strode back up to the house without once looking back, her spine stiff and straight. Only when she was hidden by hibiscus and frangipani bushes did she risk a peek. He was already some distance up the beach, walking with that smooth panther's gait, tall and erect against the dazzling sand and the glowing, incandescent blue of the lagoon. Her treacherous bones turned to honey. Jerking herself around, she went inside, feeling profoundly foolish.

Five minutes after she had come out of the shower the telephone rang. There was no reason to suspect that it might be Hugh Bannatyne, but her voice was remote and guarded as she said, 'Hello.'

An unknown masculine voice asked, 'Miss Blair Doyle?'

'Yes,' she said cautiously.

'Miss Doyle, it's Johnny Joseph here. We met last night.'

Johnny Joseph——? After a puzzled moment Blair's frown cleared. Of course, the manager of the sports team. 'Yes, I remember.'

'Miss Doyle, we'd like you to attend a barbecue tonight on the little motu out from the hotel. The team has decided we should repay some of the superb hospitality we've received on Fala'isi, and we'd like you to come if you can possibly make it. I know it's very short notice, but some of us are going off on a cruise tomorrow so this is the last night we're all going to be together.'

Blair did not want to go to a barbecue, but she found herself saying weakly, 'That sounds super. What time?'

'About six, on the beach in front of the hotel.' He sounded pleased, and she was glad she had agreed. 'We'll see you there, then.'

Blair chose to wear separates, a gold silk wrap-around shirt with a full, floating skirt in the same material, and flat-heeled sandals in a deeper shade. She had washed her hair and brushed it straight back, holding it off her face with two slides decorated with gold starfish and shells and white and gold frangipani flowers. As she looked at herself in the mirror she wondered whether thirty was too old to wear her hair like that, but in spite of a close inspection she could see only tiny lines at the corners of her eyes.

Yet she didn't look the same as she had at twenty. A vast distance, defined by experience rather than years, separated the girl she had been then from the woman she was now. At twenty she had thought herself so sophisticated and knowledgeable, able to take on the world, whereas in reality she had been a self-centred, sheltered schoolgirl with only confidence and a certain skill at decorating for assets. Smiling wryly, she sprayed herself with Ivoire perfume and turned away.

The evening started well. The hotel had built a private entertainment area on the little island on the reef, a wide terrace bordered by Hawaiian torches and backed by a pool where gold and black koi carp swam slowly, their petulant mouths set in expressions of unfaltering satisfaction, like a woman who knew her beauty was so irresistible that she need do nothing more than exist to be admired.

In the middle was an airy pavilion with a bar and a dance-floor, its latticework sides draped with festoons of a creeping plant. The heavy, exotic scent of its scarlet flowers hung like a potent miasma in the air. To separate the area from the coconut palms and low scrub of the original vegetation some genius had set thick tropical plantings—frangipani with white flowers floating like milky stars, the huge, flamboyant trumpets of amaryllis, delicate palms and Indian night jasmine with its exquisite perfume. Over it all the sea breathed its pervasive tang.

It was the outsider's version of the South Sea Islands, artificial, flamboyant, entirely bogus, with all of the beauty and none of the very real perils of living in the

Pacific. Blair enjoyed it, but would have liked a beach barbecue on the unspoiled motu better. Still, this was what the resort was for—to give visitors a sanitised but still very beautiful illusion of the romantic tropics.

When after an hour or so the boats stopped ferrying passengers across from the beach at the hotel, Blair relaxed. Obviously the man she couldn't get out of her mind wasn't going to honour the occasion with his presence. She was flirting lightly with a magnificent male whose muscles didn't know where to stop when a swift, involuntary tug at her senses warned her that she was being watched.

Hugh had arrived. After being greeted with the subtle deference given to rich and powerful people, he stood talking to a man Blair dimly recognized as the coach. Despising herself, she dragged her attention away from him and back to the man beside her.

'I did a bit of swotting up when I found we were coming here,' he said, emboldened by the lazy warmth of her smile. 'Read a few books. One in particular was interesting. It was a history of the place. I know a lot of these Pacific islands have bloodthirsty pasts, but even for those days this place went overboard.'

Blair hoped she didn't show her surprise. Somehow she hadn't expected him to be interested in history. To her shame, she discovered that she was talking to a doctor. She responded with vivacity and interest, aware that she was using him as a shield. For all his size and poise, for all the confidence that came from knowing he was famous for his sporting skills, her companion was an ordinary man, and she was able to deal with him.

Hugh Bannatyne was another story altogether, a threat to her in some primitive, fundamental way. He was interested in her—why else would he ask if she and Sam were lovers?—yet he kept behind barriers so high that the man himself was inaccessible. A reckless part of her, left over from her rash youth, whispered tantalisingly that it would be a challenge to break through the walls to the man behind them, but the minute it presented itself she firmly squashed the idea. She was happy, or as happy as she could be, and she wasn't going to jeopardise that hard-won contentment by walking into danger.

Her companion said, 'I believe the island is beautiful. Do you think you could take pity on a man and show him some of the beauty spots?'

Cynicism flattened Blair's smile. She rather doubted that the beauty spots he wanted to explore had anything to do with the island's lush scenery. 'I'm afraid I have to work,' she said lightly, her eyes limpid green pools. 'Your best bet is to contact the hotel's tour guide and organise something. They're very good. Anyway, aren't you going on a cruise?'

He took the gentle rebuff with aplomb. 'Only some of us.'

Blair noticed two girls on the other side of the pavilion, the daughters of a New Zealand couple who were working on a three-year contract in the island. Now that the universities in New Zealand had finished for the year they had arrived back on the island for the summer holidays. Pretty and confident, they were, Blair decided, much more suitable companions for the man she was with.

Within a couple of minutes she had introduced them and was listening with every appearance of interest as they talked. Two or three more team members drifted up. Feeling dowagerish, she made more introductions. A little later, satisfied that they were all enjoying themselves, she extricated herself.

Hugh Bannatyne looked up. For a terrifying moment Blair felt like a target displayed in a sniper's sights. Then, without emotion, he nodded as though she was barely an acquaintance. Blair inclined her head graciously.

That second rejection hurt something she had thought dead years ago. God, would she never learn? Betrayed yet again by her body, by the essential part of her that looked for something complementary in a man, she hadn't been aware of spinning hopes and fancies, yet she must have been, for that deliberate, offhand dismissal was like a blade to her heart.

Of course she couldn't run away, which was her first cowardly impulse. She exchanged a few pleasantries with Sam, who was excited at the imminent prospect of his children's arrival, sat down to talk for quite a long time with Sandy MacDonald, the New Zealand-born wife of the manager of the island's biggest bank, and all the time, through the laughter and the conversation and the flaring light of the torches, she was aware of Hugh, like her, moving through the guests, doing his part to make the evening a success. In spite of the barricade he interposed between himself and the rest of the world, he had excellent manners.

Perhaps she was the only person who noticed that wall. Perhaps, she thought derisively, it wasn't really there, and that maverick, feverish attraction had set her weaving moonbeams.

The food was delicious, and the occasion all that anyone could ask for; heavy with perfume, the soft tropical night settled about them with a rush, the gleaming water in the pool reflected huge, glittering stars in a sky as matt and dark as purple velvet, and the muted roar of the combers on the reef, the quintessential sound of the Pacific, blended with the cheerful Polynesian music played by the band.

Carefully, Blair made sure that she and Hugh didn't meet at any stage. It wasn't difficult; there were enough people there to evade him successfully. Of course she was helped by the fact that he was avoiding her too.

After a dinner served from two huge tables set up on the beach, music beckoned them back into the pavilion. Blair danced with two of the visiting sportsmen, with the surgeon, with Sam, and with the young, brash sportsman she had taken an instant dislike to the preceding night. His name was Paul Swithin, one of the stars of the team, and with his cocky good looks he had clearly been spoiled. Unfortunately he'd drunk enough to release a few inhibitions that would have been the better for being caged.

Blair put up with the way he held her too close, but when his hand crept up to slide beneath her shirt she pulled herself away and said crisply, 'Keep your hands to yourself, or your friends will see how you react to a slapped face or a knee in the groin.'

Sheer shock showed in his face, to be replaced by a sullen anger. 'Who the hell do you think you are, lady?' he sneered. 'Lady Muck?'

'Someone who doesn't have to put up with your drunken gropings,' she said curtly.

Fortunately the band finished their number and she turned to walk away. But his ego wouldn't allow that. Laughing as though she had said something funny, he slid his arm around her waist and hugged her tight, not letting her go until they reached the edge of the dance-floor.

Blair's face revealed nothing of her emotions although her contempt glittered in her eyes. He said offensively, 'Thanks for nothing. Next time I dance it won't be with an iceberg.'

Her brows lifted. Quite deliberately she looked him over. 'You need to change your technique,' she said coolly, 'or you won't be dancing with anyone else. Most of these women have husbands or fathers here, and those that don't have friends.'

She swung on her heel and left him, irritated with him for being so crass and herself for reacting so violently to it. The music began to throb again, but she no longer felt like dancing, or like doing anything other than going home. A hand on her arm stopped her; she looked up, her smile set and studied, directly into the icy blue eyes of Hugh Bannatyne.

CHAPTER THREE

HUGH didn't say anything, merely turned her into his arms. She went into his embrace as though that was her home, and they danced like two lovers in a dream, silent, wholly absorbed in each other.

Her instincts hadn't played her false. Slowly, gracefully, they moved in unison, his long leg parting hers when they turned, their steps harmonising perfectly. Blair had been told often enough by love-struck friends of the subtle, potent messages that bypassed the brain and homed straight to the sensitive parts of the body, but until that moment she had never believed in their existence. Now, in this man's arms, they raced through her, setting each nerve and cell on fire.

Her senses were heightened, intensified, as though she had been given some sort of drug; his scent, faint, teasing, an erotic amalgam of musk and salt, with a hidden trace that had to be the basic odour of his masculinity, tormented her. It cut through the defences she had built so carefully around her emotions, sliced right through to her heart, so that she thought she could taste him on her lips, on her tongue.

Through her lashes she saw his hand, the lean, bronzed fingers curled loosely yet with purpose around the slender length of hers. His chest rose and fell, a delicious, startling friction against the soft flesh of her breasts; lassitude crept sensuously through her, heating her blood, holding her in stasis, in waiting, for something she had never experienced.

She tried to struggle free of its enervating enchantment. Much less logically than usual, her brain told her that this was merely physical attraction, the call of healthy, virile male to healthy, fertile female, the battle of the sexes reduced to its most primitive component—the need to mate.

But, although she accepted that, she was still claimed by this involuntary yearning, the barely perceptible, rhythmic contractions deep inside a body that recognised something her mind was not prepared to admit.

How different this close embrace from the one with the young sportsman! That had been a gross intrusion on her privacy. This was——

Blair stiffened, realising with shock just how near she had come to an unspoken but unmistakable surrender. Instantly Hugh's arm tightened across her back, holding her prisoner. He said nothing, but she sensed an implacable determination, and for a moment an atavistic panic kicked her in the stomach.

He held her like that until the music finished. Only then did he let her go. Blair shot a quick, angry look up at the carved, angular features, met nothing but the polished sapphire screen of his gaze. Then he smiled, and suddenly she was drowning in attraction, as irresistible and devastating as a forest fire.

'Thank you,' she said, her voice precise and toneless.

'Thank *you*. You dance like a dream.'

Her smile was a model of politeness, empty, mocking. 'I was well taught.'

'But you weren't taught grace, or a sense of rhythm, or how to follow a man so well that he feels like Nureyev,' he returned, watching her with half-closed eyes.

His compliments should have excited her but they left an acid taste in her mouth. He might even mean them; it made no difference. Blair gave him the smile she used to hold people at bay. It was lazily provocative, and she made great play with sleepy eyes and long, flirtatious lashes; it meant as little as his compliments. 'But I could only do that with a magnificent dancer,' she said sweetly.

Someone called her name; she turned with barely hidden relief to a woman she knew slightly, and within a few seconds there were other people around them. After a while she was able to slip away, and for the rest of the evening she made sure they weren't in the same group again.

He knew what she was doing, of course. However, although she looked up quite often to see him watching her, he made no effort to come near her. Blair should have been relieved, but somehow his unhurried, purposeful surveillance sent a trickle of ice across her nerve-ends.

It wasn't fair to blame the evening for her weariness. That came from within, not from the circumstances. Blair smiled and flirted and laughed her warm, husky laugh, careful not to let Paul Swithin take any other advantage, although his hot, hard stare made her uneasy. It seemed that he was one of those men who took every rejection personally, a hunter who enjoyed the chase more if the prey was terrified. Well, she was old enough not to be frightened, and she could deal with him, but there was no reason to add fuel to whatever complexes he suffered from.

The party broke up about one o'clock—far too late; she had become accustomed to early nights. Even then she couldn't get away. Sam invited her and the MacDonalds to have a drink with him, and because she wasn't looking forward to going home to an empty house Blair accepted. She didn't realise until they were halfway through their nightcap that he had invited Hugh as well, but had been turned down. Blair could only be devoutly thankful.

Half an hour later she covered a yawn with her hand, and said, 'I must go, otherwise I'll never get up in the morning.'

'I'll drive you home,' Sam said.

'No, it's not necessary. I love walking down the beach at night.'

Tony MacDonald said, 'I don't think I'll ever get accustomed to the fact that there's laughably little crime here. Sandy and I still lock the house up, even though we know we don't need to.'

'It's a lovely feeling.' Blair smiled at them all. 'I'm going to enjoy walking down the beach feeling sorry for all those poor creatures who aren't on Fala'isi. Goodnight.'

Sam shrugged. 'OK, I know that tone of voice. I'll see you tomorrow.'

The beach was deserted. Blair took off her sandals and walked through the coarse sand, trying to empty her mind so that she could soak up the enormous solitude and peace of skies studded with the ageless blaze of the stars, and the sea, stretching all the way around the world, eternal, ever-changing, yet always the same.

Fala'isi had been a refuge, a haven; she had come here shattered and cynical, and it was only in the last few months that she had begun to recover some peace of mind, to rejoice in her new independence. She was not going to allow a man, however sexually attractive, to ruin that hard-won serenity.

Almost two-thirds of the distance home she realised she was being followed. Only mildly alarmed, she turned. As soon as he realised he'd been seen, Paul Swithin increased his speed, coming up to her with a purposeful decision that sent a sudden pang of fear through her. He was smiling in a way that told her she was in trouble.

'Let's see,' he said thickly as he came up to her, 'whether you're as stand-offish now as you were before.'

And before she had time to formulate either an answer or a defence he hauled her into his arms and kissed her, thrusting his tongue into her mouth until she gagged on the rancid taste of alcohol and anger.

Alarm flared into terror, but Blair managed to control her emotions. She didn't waste time or strength in ineffectual struggling. With a sudden co-ordinated movement she bit hard on to his tongue and brought her knee up into his groin. The taste of his blood was horrible, but even worse was that she tripped in the yielding sand as she kneed him and fell with a thud that almost winded her. Panic gripped her in its mindless embrace, for her knee had not connected properly.

Gasping and swearing, he followed her down, landing on her body with an impact that took what was left of her breath away. Blair looked up through tear-filled eyes to see him raise a fist the size of a ham. She had hurt him, but she hadn't disabled him. And he was aroused; she could feel the ugly bulge pressing against her stomach.

'You bitch!' he muttered, and punched downwards.

Instinct brought her arm up to block the blow. With a convulsive heave she twisted so violently that his fist missed her face, smashing into the sand a fraction of an inch away. She had just opened her mouth to scream at the top of her voice when a shadow plucked him off her effortlessly, and hit him so hard that she thought she, too, felt the battering collision of fist with flesh and bone.

Goggling, her breath searing painfully through her lungs, she watched his body fly through the air and crumple like a bag of sawdust on to the sand.

Blair wasn't surprised when the shadow turned into Hugh Bannatyne. With cruel hands he pulled her on to her feet, holding her away so that he could see her face. His own was like that of a devil, primeval in its ferocity, frightening her far more than Paul Swithin's attack. Visions of Viking berserkers flashed into Blair's brain, and she shuddered.

She had wondered whether he would lose that mask of control when he was making love; obscurely it hurt to see it replaced by a blind, unthinking fury.

'Are you all right?' he demanded, each word explosive with aggression.

'Yes.' But she sagged, and he caught her, supporting her against the hard length of his body. It was electrifying but risky to lie against the heated strength of him. After a moment she pulled away. 'I'm all right,' she said thinly, swallowing. 'Thank you.'

As she turned towards her house he said sharply, 'Sit down, Blair.'

She was shaking, the whole world spinning around her in a hideous phantasmagoria, but she managed to retain enough control to say, 'I'm fine.'

'I'll walk you home first.'

'No! He didn't hurt me. Just get him out of here, will you?'

Swearing under his breath, Hugh picked her up and carried her across the yielding sand.

Blair croaked, 'I'm too heavy to carry up the steps.'

She might as well have saved her breath. He didn't put her down until they reached the terrace, where he deposited her on the sofa. 'Give me your keys,' he ordered, holding out his hand.

'It's not locked.' She stood up. He was sweating slightly, and she stepped back, her insides contracting at the fresh, salty scent.

'Inside, then.'

'Hugh, it isn't——'

'Blair,' he said with grim emphasis, 'don't be an idiot. I'm not going until you're all right.'

Her chin tilted. 'I am all right. Please go.'

He hesitated, then said coldly, 'Very well.'

She was inside before he had reached the beach, heading straight for the shower, desperate to rid herself of the degradation that clung like a hideous film. Half an hour later she had showered and changed and washed her hair, and was crouched on the sofa, telling herself that it was just shock, it would go away soon. But she couldn't stop shaking, even though she clenched both her teeth and her hands.

When Hugh walked in she wasn't even surprised. Touching her dry lips with the tip of her tongue, she whispered, 'What do you want?'

'I told you I'd make sure you were all right.' Vivid blue eyes searched her face. 'Have you had anything to drink?'

'No. I feel sick.'

'I'm not surprised,' he said savagely, 'but if you have tea with sugar it will help. Get into bed and I'll bring it in to you.'

Docilely she obeyed, and was sitting against her pillows clad in a pale green cotton nightgown, watching the doorway with eyes still dilated by a fear that had been long in incubation, when he appeared there with a tray.

He looked, she thought with an odd, defeated detachment, almost familiar, as though she had both known and trusted him for a long time. The violent, barbaric fury that had frightened her on the beach was gone as though it had never existed; he had had time to reimpose the control that was such an essential part of his character.

'What happened to Paul Swithin?' she asked, surprising herself with the question.

'I marched him down to the hotel and knocked up his manager.'

'Will he——?' Unable to go on, she swallowed, afflicted by a flood of sick panic.

Strangely enough Hugh seemed to know what was worrying her. 'He'll be locked in his room all night, but just in case I'll stay here with you. Drink this up.' He put the tray on the bedside table.

The tea was warm and sweet and milky, and she drank it obediently until the tears frozen behind her eyes melted and she began to cry.

'Blair,' he said harshly. 'Blair, don't...'

'I'm sorry, it's stupid——' But try as she did she couldn't stop.

He sat down on the bed and took her into his arms, holding her close. Blair knew she was playing with fire, that she should let him go, but she clung, burying her face in his wide, reassuring shoulder, and wept until finally, the shock dissipated, she subsided into sleep.

She woke towards dawn, warmer than she had been for years, the icy centre of her heart thawed. A small smile curved her mouth. She knew who was with her in the bed, in the heavy darkness. Cuddled against him, his arm under her neck, she lay with her head on his shoulder. His breathing was regular, without impediment.

A bird called, its liquid notes dripping through the air, sweet, exotic yet evocative. According to the islanders, if two people heard the tikau bird together they were doomed to fall in love. It was a charming little legend, and of course Blair didn't believe a word of it, but somehow it set the seal on her happiness.

Still smiling, she ran a light finger across Hugh's wide expanse of chest. Hair like silk curled around her finger, the skin beneath as smooth and flexible as the finest glove leather.

Everything that had happened to her in the last three years had been banished, the trauma eased, by the mere fact of sleeping with this intensely guarded man. She should, she thought dreamily, get the hell out of the bed while she could, but she wasn't going to.

This had all the inevitability of fate.

'Don't do that,' he said, his beautiful voice husky with sleep.

'Why?'

'Because I might think you want more than just comfort.'

For answer, she lifted herself on to an elbow and smiled into his face, letting her ruffled hair fall around it like a curtain. He looked at her with eyes as brilliant and clear as the jewels they resembled, translucent as the dawn sky, no longer concealing the desire she had sensed since that first meeting, the hidden flame of hunger, of passion.

'And you'd be right,' she said, the last word whispered against the clear-cut line of his mouth.

He resisted only a second. As her hand moved across his chest, spreading wide until she could feel the solid, rapidly speeding beat of his heart beneath her palm, the tip of her tongue traced his lips with delicate, dangerous precision, outlining the top lip, then the more sweeping arc of the bottom.

He groaned deep in his throat and his arms came up and caught her, iron bands around a pliant, yielding body, and pulled her over him so that she could feel his taut strength, the need and passion in him, as wild as the desire that throbbed through her.

It was like nothing she had ever experienced before, nothing in her whole life. It was consuming fire, and primitive savagery, and a strange, fiery tenderness. He touched her as though he had never had a woman before, with such devouring yearning that she couldn't help but respond, yet his experience showed in his insight into her needs, the sensual expertise of his hands and his mouth on her skin.

Blair was experienced too, but her response was so astonishingly pristine and new-fledged that she was racked by the age-old shyness of a virgin. This was something she had never expected to discover, this unknown territory of the senses.

Hugh's breath hissed between his teeth when she curved her hand around his hip and pulled him close against her so that, mouth joined to mouth, their bodies were welded together by the fire leaping from one to the other.

When he entered her it was with a fierce elemental passion, a need to take and imprint himself that she understood for she too wanted to mark him for life with her hunger, so that if ever another woman lay with him like this he would see only Blair's face, feel only the sleek warmth of her body beneath him and around him, holding him prisoner forever.

Blair thought she knew about making love, about sex, about the myriad ways there were for a man and a woman to pleasure each other, but nothing in her life had prepared her for this. Ecstasy, simple and keen as a lance, shook her, held her pinioned, stabbed her with an unbearable agony of delight, until at last it was over, and she was shaking, her vision blurred with tears, so totally removed from reality that she couldn't even find words to think with.

Almost immediately the same dark compulsion gripped him, arching his lean, bronzed body. His head drew back, his features became stark with fulfilment as he spilled himself into her in the same unbelievable rapture, then collapsed, their breath commingling, bodies sleek with sweat and satiation.

When he went to move Blair made a little murmur of protest. But he moved anyway, rolling away from her and on to his back, his forearm over his eyes. Then he swung his long legs over the bed.

'Do you have to go?' she asked lazily.

'Yes.' One word, but that was all that was needed to smash her unformed dreams into shards.

Slowly, making a production of it, she pulled the sheet up before turning her head to look at him, her green eyes dazed and smoky with unasked questions.

'You've got what you wanted,' he said coldly. 'Don't blame me if it didn't live up to your expectations.'

'Oh, it more than lived up to expectations.' How cool her voice, how calm and even! 'You have a great natural talent for lovemaking, as I'm sure your other one-night stands have told you. Thank you for sharing it with me.'

He was pulling on his shirt, his fingers quick and deft as they did up the buttons. Blair closed her eyes. Those same hands had worshipped her body, slid across her skin as though they loved it, those hands had wrung a desperate, gasping response from her.

Humiliation washed over her, a debilitating flood; she fought it back. She would not allow him to make her ashamed of her frank surrender to her sexuality, the way she had given him everything that she was, everything she could be.

* * *

He left the same day. There were three flights each week from Fala'isi to New Zealand, two that left at the unearthly hour of four-thirty in the morning, the third six hours later at the much more civilised time of ten o'clock. It was characteristic that Hugh should be able to leave on the later one, which was usually booked out; he had the arrogant confidence of a man who had fate on his side. Or perhaps he had pulled strings.

Blair knew about his departure because she was told by the manager and coach of the team when they arrived at her house just before lunch, profuse with apologies. Ironically, Paul Swithin had left on the same flight, his passage out organised immediately after Hugh had told the team management what had happened.

'He should keep off alcohol,' Blair said, her voice cool and emotionless, when they had told her this. 'He seemed all right when we danced together, crass but in control. He'd had a lot more to drink when he assaulted me.'

The two men exchanged glances. 'It's not the first time we've had an incident involving the same man,' the coach admitted uncomfortably. 'And yes, last time it happened after he'd been drinking. He promised that it would never happen again, but obviously we're going to have to think very carefully about what this will do to his prospects as a representative of New Zealand. I can't say how sorry we are, Miss Doyle. I hope you aren't too upset about the—what happened. If there's anything we can do—I thought perhaps a doctor——'

'No, I'm all perfectly right.' Paul Swithin's attack, ugly and alarming though it had been, no longer had the power to frighten her. What was upsetting her had nothing to do with the sportsman. She went on, 'Thanks for taking the time to tell me he's gone. It certainly isn't your fault he can't handle alcohol or rejection.'

'You're very kind.'

But they still looked uncomfortable, and eventually she realised they were worried in case she contacted the Press. By the time she'd reassured them that the last thing she intended to do was tell anyone about the sordid little episode it was lunchtime, and the one ambition she had left was to crawl back into bed and stay incommunicado for several days. Months. Years, even.

However, clearly wanting to do something for her, they asked her to lunch, and because she understood their feelings—and because if she stayed at home she was going to do nothing but stare at the walls and remember—she accepted.

In spite of all their efforts it was a tense meal. Although the food tasted of nothing, Blair ate everything on her plate, made mechanical, polite conversation, even drank a glass of wine. The surface courtesy her mother had drilled into her helped push Hugh to the back of her mind, and gloss over the pain and humiliation.

When she had finished her coffee she felt free to make her departure. She was not to get away so easily, however. Halfway across the foyer she was hailed by Sandy MacDonald and one of her friends.

'Come and have a drink,' Sandy said enthusiastically. 'We're just about to settle down for a good old gossip about last night!'

Blair produced a bleak little smile. 'Sorry,' she said, 'but I've got a wretched headache.'

'Yes, you do look washed out.' Sandy produced an arch smile. 'Exhaustion, perhaps? You and that absolutely magnificent Bannatyne man walked home together, I understand. Was he waiting for you when you left us last night? You lucky devil. I wish I were twenty years younger, and I'd give you a run for your money!'

Ignoring the younger woman's hissed, 'Sandy!' Blair said meaninglessly, 'Yes, he was very nice. See you later,' and left them.

Why did she feel so shattered, as though her life had been mauled and broken by a careless hand? She wasn't in love with the man; God knows, she thought despairingly, I don't believe in love any longer!

What they had shared was just sex. Good sex, admittedly, the best she'd ever experienced. Her eyes turned the cloudy green of the lagoon after rain as her treacherous memory reminded her of just how good it had been.

But love had nothing to do with it. It was an overwhelming physical attraction, purely a matter of hormones and basic, unemotional hungers. Hugh had even helped her; in a way she supposed she should be thankful to both him and Paul Swithin. If it hadn't been for the trauma on the beach she wouldn't have lost her self-control and wept, and if that hadn't happened Hugh wouldn't have stayed.

And if he hadn't stayed she wouldn't have woken in the morning and wanted to make love...

It had been almost three years, and all that time she had been convinced that she would never again feel safe enough with any man to lower her guard. The therapist had told her that it would probably come, that she needed to relax, that time would eventually work its miracle. But Gerald hadn't waited.

Now Blair could feel the honeyed tide of sensuality running fresh, more strong than it had ever been, and that was almost entirely due to Hugh Bannatyne, who made love as though he'd been born for it, tender yet fierce, and at the end found his iron-clad self-sufficiency breached by a desire so intense he couldn't control it.

Yes, she should be grateful to him.

She was depressed because they hadn't used any protection, so she could be pregnant. And in this day and age it wasn't just foolish to indulge in one-night stands with a stranger, it was downright dangerous.

Yet somehow she couldn't worry about that. There had been something almost driven about Hugh, something famished, as though he had been celibate for a long time.

Blair bit her lip. Perhaps he too was careful not to indulge in affairs with strangers. Possibly he was even now wondering rather sickly whether those maddened hours had put his future on the line.

Back at the house she couldn't settle to anything, not even to the souvenirs. 'I am not going to let a man put me off my work,' she told her studio defiantly. Then she realised she was staring at the three oils Hugh had bought. What was going to happen to them now? Would he cancel the cheque?

Like a woman stretching out a hand to a snake, she turned to the one of the arid hills of El Amir. Her teeth bit into her bottom lip as she looked at it. The brooding menace, the atmosphere of age and intense, malevolent heat and dryness were still there, but somehow the sting had been taken from it.

Tears burned beneath her lashes. With a sniff she picked up the slightly crumpled photograph of a head-stone, lonely in its Sydney graveyard so far from this idyllic place, and began to reproduce it.

It was almost as though the simple act of copying a photograph unleashed something inside her, some block. She painted for the rest of the day and long into the night, and through the next week, swept up in a fervour of creativity.

This work was not pretty souvenirs for tourists. Everything she painted was a tribute to the South Seas, to the lushness and beauty of the place, its danger, and the hint of otherworldliness, the expectation of something just beyond the horizon, waiting to be discovered, beckoning, ever-alluring, ultimately even more seductive than the beauty and glamour of the islands.

That expectation had bedazzled everyone who sailed the South Pacific, luring the Polynesians almost all the way to South America, persuading them ever on in spite of the manifold ways to die on its broad waters, and after them had come others, ending only a couple of hundred years ago with the Europeans who'd thought they'd found paradise in the warm waters and ravishing islands and golden people. Like her, they had learned that, for all its beauty, paradise could be a lost and lonely place, a place where peril was inextricably mixed with beauty.

When, exhausted and smelling of paint, she finally laid down her brush, she stood looking at her work with eyes that were gritty yet searching. The lagoon shimmered on the canvas, a hackneyed subject saved, she hoped, from cliché by the depth of the emotion that throbbed beneath the superficial glamour.

This one was, she thought dispassionately, like its immediate predecessors, better than anything else she had done. Better than the El Amir ones, better than the canvases she had produced when she was back in New Zealand, trying desperately to convey what she needed from and loved in her country.

Another thing she should thank Hugh Bannatyne for? So why did despair clog her throat, ache in her heart? 'Because you're a fool,' she said aloud, turning away.

The telephone made her jump. Something perilously like hope sparkling in her smile, she answered it. For a moment the hope soared phoenix-like as she realised it was an overseas call, but it died as soon as she heard Tegan Sinclair's voice. Which was bad, because Tegan was her oldest and best friend.

'Hi,' she said, striving for normality. 'When did you stop writing letters? What's going on?'

When Tegan laughed, Blair knew. 'Blair, it's the most wonderful news and you are only the fourth person to know after Kieran and my parents. I'm pregnant!'

Envy clawed hideously. Blair knew by now that she wasn't having Hugh Bannatyne's baby. Of course she was glad, very relieved, but some part of her grieved obstinately. Her biological clock must be ticking, she thought sardonically as she forced the appropriate note of delight into her answer. 'Wonderful! How are you?'

'Radiant, my dear. Oh, Blair, I'm so happy! And Kieran is over the moon!'

'I'll just bet he is. Hey, am I going to be godmother, or is there a better candidate?'

'There couldn't be a better candidate,' Tegan said firmly. 'You are hereby invited, or subpoenaed, or whatever it is one does to godparents. Are you all right? You sound a bit odd.'

It had always been impossible to put anything over Tegan. She had been the first to realise that Blair was not going to get over her experiences in El Amir easily, and she and her handsome husband had been towers of strength in the following months when Blair's marriage had fallen apart under the strain.

'No, nothing's wrong,' Blair said hastily. 'Everything's fine, actually. I've just spent all night finishing what I think is the best thing I've ever done, and I'm tired.'

There was silence, before Tegan said on a half-sigh, 'I suppose I hoped that this was just going to be a passing phase, and that eventually you'd come home and buy back into the firm. But it's not, and you're not, are you?'

'No. Oh, I've wondered; in fact ever since I came up here I thought perhaps I was just fooling myself, running away from everything, but—Tegan, this is *good*. I was right to stop decorating houses and try this. Eventually I'll come home, but I won't ever be part of Decorators Inc again.'

'Then there's nothing more to be said.' Tegan's wry smile was mirrored in her voice. 'I'm so pleased it's working out for you, but I never expected it not to come right, really—you have such vast amounts of determination!'

'Determination is one thing, talent is another.'

Tegan sounded shocked. 'Idiot, we all knew you had the talent! That series you did on El Amir gave me the willies, and you know Kieran wanted to buy them. Distinctly uncomfortable, he called them, but certainly an investment.'

Blair grinned. 'Oh, and Kieran, a merchant banker to his fingertips, knows whether I'm an artist or not?'

Tegan's warm laughter echoed down the line. 'Kieran knows everything,' she said. 'Not that I tell him, of course.'

'Of course not.' Tegan and her husband were wholly besotted with each other. Repressing another ignoble pang of envy, Blair asked, 'So what are you going to do with the business now, little mother?'

'Keep it going. I'd go mad sitting around at home being a lady, but I'll have to ease up quite a bit. Apart from anything else, Kieran's gone all protective. I'll ask Andrea if she wants to work with me.'

'Andrea? Not the Andrea who's Kieran's sister, surely?'

'Yes, I know you think she's unstable, but she's been fine since—well, since even before she and Rick got married; and she really is good, Blair. She hasn't come right out and asked if she could work for me, but she's been taking university extension classes on all sorts of interesting and useful things like art appreciation, as well as asking me about the business every chance she gets, so I think now is a good time. After all, she won't dare upset the mother of her future niece or nephew, will she?'

Blair, who remembered Kieran's sister to be a difficult, rather haughty woman, pulled a face, but said mildly enough, 'I'll grant you she's got talent. Good luck with her. And you take care of my godchild!'

They talked for some time further. When Blair put the receiver down she almost stumbled under a weariness of the spirit that made her blink back tears. It was stupid to feel so bereft. Tegan was very happy with her husband, and the news of her pregnancy made Blair happy too; her restlessness was probably because it had followed so closely the news of that other baby, her ex-husband's, the child he had always said he didn't want, didn't need.

However, that didn't explain why in the following weeks she dreamed of Hugh Bannatyne every night, and woke each morning with tears in her heart.

Perhaps she just needed a man.

If that was so, she was going to have to learn to do without one. Apart from Hugh, she had only ever made love to the two men she'd loved. It was, she thought, strangely ironic that Hugh, whom she didn't love, had been the only one able to reach that hitherto hidden part of her, the white-hot, primeval source of passion that had captured her so effectively that she couldn't struggle free of its tempting trap.

She drifted into an erotic dream, or perhaps an erotic memory, her mouth curving softly as she remembered how magnificent he had been, as sleek and bold and lusty as any bronze god from the days when no maiden was safe from their advances...

'Oh, God!' she groaned, getting abruptly to her feet. 'Get out of my head!'

Unfortunately it wasn't easy to dislodge him. He seemed to have taken up permanent residence there. In an effort to work through her memories and rob them of power she painted him as she remembered him, arched above her, his head flung back in the agonised ecstasy of his climax, each sinew and tendon and muscle in his beautiful body taut and harshly delineated with the force of his passion.

The attempted exorcism didn't work. It was another painting she'd never be able to sell, another to put in her private archives. She should destroy it, but she wouldn't.

A couple of days later her bank statement arrived, the balance nicely plumped by the amount of his cheque. In a quandary, she wondered whether she should ask Sam for Hugh's home address so that she could send the canvases on to him. It would, she thought, be damned awkward. How could she explain that he had just walked off? And Sam probably wouldn't tell her, anyway. Almost certainly it would be against the resort's policy.

The paintings remained in the studio, hidden from sight.

Thoroughly sick of her own company, Blair accepted invitations to parties she didn't want to go to, and spent several evenings castigating herself for not enjoying them. After that she accepted no more invitations until one arrived from Tamsyn Chapman, fresh back from England only a week before. She and her husband were giving a large, informal evening reception for a group of Japanese businessmen.

Blair accepted. It would not do to get on the wrong side of a man who could send her back to New Zealand. And if at the back of her mind she knew that she wanted to keep in contact, however distant, with Hugh, she refused to admit it.

Asa descended on the house one evening, demanding some more pictures for her shop. Blair spent a week producing them, then embarked on several big canvases. She focused on the steep, savage mountains of the interior, hiring a four-wheel-drive vehicle to travel rugged side-roads, exploring places that normally she would never have dared visit. She was working harder than she ever had in her life, and most of the results she was moderately pleased with.

Two months after Hugh had left, and two days before the Chapmans' party, she was sitting on the terrace in the slow heat of a tropical evening when she finally admitted that she wasn't going to be able to forget him.

The sun had just set in a blaze of pure, clear scarlet, and for a second as it dipped over the edge of the world a flash of exquisite green flared out. Blair's breath locked in her throat. If only she could paint it sincerely, honestly, giving the experience its due weight. If only she had Hugh here to share the experience with.

She shifted restlessly in the deep wicker chair. Damn the man, he sneaked into her thoughts far too often.

She missed him.

Oh, she wasn't in love with him. How could you be in love with a man you didn't know? Hugh was so detached, so much in command of his emotions, so self-contained, that she knew nothing of the real man behind the copper mask.

Except that when he made love, her memory reminded her slyly, that control was shattered as if it had never existed.

Tension compelled her to her feet and out across the coarse grass. Sina's husband had cut it that day and the scent was fresh and pleasing. The scarlet glow in the sky was fading, the spear of emerald light had disappeared as fast as it had come, and so far only one brilliant star clung like a pendant in the rapidly darkening sky.

The coral stone balustrade was warm beneath Blair's hands. She stared along the beach towards the lights of the resort, searching for something she refused to accept, her heart aching with emptiness.

Before her incredulous eyes Hugh materialised out of the thickening darkness, tall, arrogantly poised, striding along the smooth curve of the beach like a conqueror.

Blair couldn't run back to the dubious safety of the house, couldn't drag her eyes off him. A bewildering variety of emotions tightened her throat as her hands clenched on to the sun-warmed stone.

'What are you doing here?' she asked harshly when he stopped at the foot of the steps.

'Are you pregnant?'

His voice was almost uninterested, yet there was a note in it that demanded an answer. Disappointment, hard and obdurate as stone, rolled over her. Blair said sharply, 'No, I'm not, and a letter would have done, thank you.'

'I don't think so,' he said distantly as he came up the steps from the beach.

Blair had no time for women who fainted or cried or had hysterics, but at this moment she understood their reasons for reacting that way. The quick stab of anger was overtaken by a deep, terrifying joy at seeing him again; contempt was followed by fear that she might not be able to resist the forbidden temptations he represented, and a hidden excitement throbbed through her in a drum-roll of anticipation. Fainting seemed a fairly practical way of dealing with the situation.

It was not Blair's way, however. 'Well, you know now,' she said brusquely, 'so you can go.'

'So arrogant,' he said, sounding amused. 'I've flown all the way up here——'

She managed to produce an offhand shrug. 'There was no need for you to do that. As I said, a letter would have done. I'm perfectly well, I assure you.'

'Good. In that case, can I persuade you to ask me in for a drink? Or just to talk?'

'No.'

'I don't intend to take you to bed,' he said. His voice, his tone were perfectly composed, yet a thread of steel in the words hinted at an inflexible will.

Irrationally disappointed, she retorted, 'You haven't got a hope, so if that's what you came back for you're completely out of luck. Believe me, I'm not usually so easily persuaded as I was last time.'

It was still light enough for her to see his brows rise. 'I don't recollect having to persuade you at all,' he said mockingly. 'Your frank, open need is something I've often remembered. Were you just so frightened by that hoon's assault that you needed reassurance?'

Outraged, she spluttered, 'No!'

'So why did you seduce me, then?'

She said angrily, 'This is the weirdest conversation, and we shouldn't be having it.'

'Why?'

The word lashed out like a whip. Embarrassed, Blair shook her head. 'Because—oh, because I just want to forget about the whole thing.'

'Can you?' Silence, until he said roughly, 'I can't.'

She wasn't going to pursue that, or give him any opening to enlarge on it. Her mouth was so dry that she had to moisten it before she could ask, 'Why did you come back?'

His shoulders moved, as though her bluntness surprised him. 'I suppose I felt under some sort of obligation,' he said at last. 'If you were pregnant then I'd have to help. A letter seemed—impolite.'

The onrushing stars, sparkling and huge, cast enough light to limn his strong, angular features. They were devoid of emotion. Blair turned away. Impolite? It was an odd choice of word, but at least he seemed prepared to stand by his actions.

He said quickly, 'And because there's something unfinished.'

'Don't be silly.' The words were as cutting and scornful as she could make them, curt syllables falling like ice cubes into the warm, melting night. 'What we had was a one-night stand. It was good, but that was all it was. The very essence of a one-night stand is that nothing is expected, no commitment——'

'Blair,' he said, that hateful amusement back in his tone, 'you're talking through a hole in your head. If it was simply a one-night stand why are you so angry with me, and why am I back here?'

'You've just admitted you'd feel responsible if I was pregnant,' she said brusquely.

'Well, you allow me a sense of responsibility, at least. I suppose I should be thankful for that.'

'I don't want your gratitude for anything. I've told you I'm not pregnant, so you can go away again.'

'Why?'

She began to say that she didn't want him there, then fell silent.

Inexorably he said, 'You're a sophisticated woman, able and accustomed, I imagine, to deal reasonably with your past lovers. But you're not being reasonable now. Why are you afraid?'

'I am not!' She swung around, green eyes glittering as she scanned his face. 'I just don't want you here.'

'Very well, then,' he said coolly, although she could see the way his mouth twisted, and there was something frightening in the gleam of his eyes beneath their dark, thick lashes.

Before she had time to react his hands fastened on to her shoulders. Blair stared up into an implacable face, its harsh contours lovingly delineated by the moonlight. 'No,' she said, but her voice was a whisper, and when he said deeply,

'Yes, you beautiful liar,' she closed her eyes in despair.

The kiss was gentle at first, gentle enough for Blair to wonder whether he was trying to prove something, but almost instantly they caught fire from each other, and by the time it finished she was pressed fiercely against him, her hands hard across his back, offering him all that he wanted.

'God,' he muttered, his mouth touching the long line of her neck, not just once but several times, the brief, fiery graze of his lips sending wild little shudders through her whole body. 'I didn't intend this to happen——'

He didn't try to pull away but she tightened her arms anyway, and he laughed beneath his breath, a husky sound that melted her backbone.

'Blair,' he said, making her name a caress that sighed along her nerves, 'does this mean you want another one-night stand? Because if you do I can't refuse you. Only you'd better know now that it will be followed by another and another and another, until I've taught you to use a different term to describe our relationship. Is that what you want?'

She had been watching his mouth as he talked, the chiselled contours of it, the small upward lift at the corners, the way it almost softened when he said her name. Now her gaze wandered, tracing the arrogant slash of a jaw, the strongly modelled cheekbones, until it was captured by eyes that gleamed strangely beneath heavy, half-lowered lashes.

Her stomach lurched. For an incredible moment she thought she was being swallowed up by those eyes, drowning in their heated sensuality, burned by the flames she saw in them, blue as the hottest flame above a candle.

In a thread of a voice, she asked, 'What do you do to me?'

'I don't know, but you make me lose control so completely that I don't even think about the cost.' He spoke angrily, his voice harsh and proud.

It took an immense effort of will to look away. It hurt to force her arms loose, to draw back and stand up without the support of his lean body. Blair had never known that she could be swamped by weakness, yet not want to resist it. She felt as though she had been taken over by an alien will. It frightened her, gave her the strength to say unevenly, 'I wish you hadn't come back.'

'Would you have forgotten?'

She pressed her teeth down on to her trembling, slightly swollen mouth. 'Yes,' she lied, her tone giving her away entirely.

His smile was taunting. 'Just as easily as I'd have forgotten you,' he said.

She was stronger now, his response whipping up a spark of determination. He'd said he hadn't come back to take up where he'd left off, but that kiss had marked him a liar, too. No doubt he thought he'd have a willing bedmate for the next few nights, and then he'd leave her again. And that way lay danger, a danger so immense that she didn't know its dimensions; she had only her woman's intuition to warn her off.

Vaguely aware that she was being unfair, she said unevenly, 'It doesn't mean anything. I don't want to see you again.'

He stood for a long moment looking down into her intransigent face, his own shuttered, angular with an intense, primitive beauty that didn't hide the frustration beneath.

'I think you're probably very wise,' he said, and there was something so derisory, so savagely contemptuous in his expression that she stepped back. 'Goodbye, Blair.'

And walking silently, leaving her as he had come to her, like a creature of the night he went back into the darkness.

CHAPTER FOUR

LATER, vigorously brushing her hair, Blair gazed out across the lagoon and tried to persuade herself to be thankful he hadn't tried to talk her into bed. She might vow to withstand his practised temptation, but she had only to touch her mouth, now soft and red, to know that she couldn't.

He cast some sort of spell on her, an enchantment that bypassed the logic and common sense she had always been rather proud of, and locked straight into some unregenerately elemental, all-consuming part of her.

She had heard of *femmes fatales*. She was afraid that she wanted an *homme fatale*.

Shivering, her body aching but her mind convinced that she had done the right thing in turning him away, she put the hairbrush down and went to bed, to lie sleepless for the rest of the night.

Why had he come back? In the light of that kiss there was only one answer. He wanted an affair. Blair shuddered. Oh, God, it was only too easy to imagine just how fulfilling an affair with him would be, and how ultimately empty. She was not a woman who liked sex for its own sake. She needed to know that she loved and was loved; for her, sex was the natural extension of shared emotions. That was why she had been so sickened by the experience in El Amir, why it had had such a profound effect on her.

And yet, she reminded herself, she had not been raped in El Amir. The chieftain who had made off with her had acted with integrity according to his culture; he'd seen their relationship as sanctified by custom. Of course he had taken no notice of her protests, but he had seen to it that she was prepared for the honour he granted her, providing her with two tutors—an older woman and a younger one who could speak a form of English. They had put her through a swift but intensive course on sensuality.

Thanks to him, Blair knew enough about the esoteric byways of sex to fill an encyclopaedia. Specifically, she had been taught how to arouse and satisfy a man.

Outrage and fear had made Blair uncooperative and antagonistic, but with unfailing good humour and a simple pragmatism that had upset her more than anything else because it had made the whole nightmarish situation seem inevitable, even normal, her tutors had worn her down. To conserve her energy she had listened, done the exercises they had insisted on, and hidden her furious resentment and fear behind a blank expression.

The exercises she still did; her doctor in New Zealand had said they were an excellent workout for her entire body, inside and out.

Fortunately, before she had been forced to use all this knowledge as a member of the harem, Kieran Sinclair had come to rescue her, like a knight on a magnificent Arab stallion. It had turned out just the way it did in fairy-tales, Blair thought with a bitter-sweet smile, only he hadn't been her prince, he was Tegan's.

The experience had left scars, some so deep that she was convinced she'd never be free of them. Even now she couldn't stand being in a room with no windows, a room where she couldn't let in the fresh, sweet air.

And the fear, the anger and bitterness at being treated as though her wishes were of no interest to anyone, had been impossible to shake off. So was the unspoken but implicit insinuation that her only value was as a beautiful, desirable body. Her sexuality had been driven underground by the experience; when she'd got back to New Zealand she had frozen every time Gerald came near her.

For some time she had blamed the break-up of her marriage on her imprisonment, but it was not so simple.

There had been something wrong already, otherwise Gerald would have waited for her to regain her confidence. Instead, he had tumbled headlong into love with a girl just out of high school.

Blair turned away sharply, pushing her hair up from her hot neck. It was past, it was over and done with; she was no longer married to Gerald, no longer in love with him. Her resentment at being made to look a fool had finally dissipated. She could, she thought wryly, even wish him well. Perhaps that was because she now knew how little of her sexuality Gerald had been able to arouse.

Hugh Bannatyne's unashamed desire had summoned a like response, freeing her from the past. Blair frowned, tracing a carved greenstone bird with her forefinger. She didn't feel her usual pleasure in its sensuous, satisfying shape and texture. Hugh had done more than release the blocked wellspring of her passion; he had taught her that there were raptures she had never before experienced.

A tide of soft apricot flooded her skin as she recalled some of them. He was a magnificent lover, strong yet tender, fierce yet controlled until that last minute when his restraint had shattered in a tide of hunger he hadn't been able to deny. And what he didn't know about a woman's body, her needs, was insignificant. Great natural talent? Or immense experience?

Blair didn't know, and she didn't care, she reminded herself crisply, jerking herself out of a far too vivid daydream. An affair was out; that night together had been an aberration. Now, his conscience satisfied, he was no doubt heading back to New Zealand. She hoped so, anyway. She didn't want to risk meeting him again.

Memories of El Amir prompted her last thought before exhaustion claimed her. Somehow she would have to see to it that he got the canvases he had paid for.

It was a measure of her confusion that she smiled as sleep claimed her.

Refusing to admit even to herself that she was afraid of running into him, she spent the next day at home, fighting restlessness and a strange sense of dislocation.

Half an hour before Sam was due to collect her for the Chapmans' party she was still wondering what on earth one wore to a reception at the house of a sort of unofficial tropical prince. Informal it might be, but Blair didn't make the mistake of thinking that a skirt and a pretty T-shirt would do.

In the end she chose an outfit in oyster-white cheesecloth, a camisole beneath a tie-fronted shirt, and long trousers that showed off the length of her legs. With it she wore earrings like a waterfall at sunset, and a gold chain belt. Sandals the same colour as the cheesecloth looked good on her narrow feet.

Her hair she brushed back off her face and anchored in place with a wide cheesecloth bandeau embroidered scantily with gold thread.

It was not normal for her to be so strung-up. The Chapmans had been kind to her, and she enjoyed their company, so why this hollow feeling in her midriff, this taut feeling of waiting for something awful but inevitable to happen? In some parts of New Zealand she'd say an earthquake was on its way, but Fala'isi didn't have earthquakes, the vulcanism that had given the island its central mountains having long since died away.

Sam certainly had no pangs of foreboding. 'I don't know what it is,' he said, eyeing her with open appreciation, 'but you seem to make most other women look too carefully finished, if you know what I mean.'

Picking up her bag, Blair grinned. 'That I'm untidy?'

'No!' He lifted his brows and shrugged, assuming a mock-disconsolate face. 'Trust me to put my foot in it. No, you just look easy, and relaxed, and so beautiful that somehow grooming doesn't come into it. Lots of women look stunning but you can see the effort it took them to get there, whereas it doesn't show with you.'

Touched, she laughed as she went out with him into the swift purple dusk. 'You've a nice line in compliments, Sam. Thank you. How are the kids enjoying their holidays?'

'They're having a marvellous time.'

His children were always a safe topic with Sam—he missed them unbearably during term when they were with their mother in Australia. As they drove through the scented tropical night he told her of their latest exploits, his voice proud and loving. Blair envied him his anchors to reality, to the future.

The Chapmans welcomed them with smiles. Grant Chapman, a tall, dark man with hawkish features, was his usual sophisticated self; his wife, however, seemed a little distracted. It didn't stop her from being as charming and friendly as she always was, but Blair was sure she could sense a certain ambivalence in her attitude——

Which was ridiculous; she was just letting the fact that Hugh was a friend of theirs distort her perceptions.

They lived in an old, low, rambling house built of coral limestone, set in beautiful gardens on a hillside above the lagoon. A mixture of antiques collected together over the years combined very successfully with good modern furniture, and the new paint made the perfect background for furniture and a carefully selected collection of *objets d'art*. Blair whole-heartedly approved.

Tonight the party was mostly out on the wide, shaded terrace that ran almost the entire length of one wing. It was casual and modern and very beautiful, with a view down the gentle half-mile slope to the shore.

She and Sam had been circulating for about five minutes when she saw Hugh, big and dark and lithely masculine. When the drumming in her head eased, Blair found that her fist was clenched beneath her heart as though she had been winded. She had spent the last two months missing him with a deep, aching hunger, and the past day wondering whether she had been a coward to whistle away the heated passion of his lovemaking, but it was patently obvious that he hadn't wasted any such time over her.

He was smiling down at a woman, and she, a pretty, vivacious creature with a riot of soft, curly black hair, was smiling back, her mouth curved in invitation, her eyes alight with excitement and interest. Blair recognised her instantly, although they had never met socially. Her photograph turned up regularly in the Australian magazines. She was Fiona Trickett, a socialite on holiday with her stepmother at some millionaire's beach cottage, and in the weeks she'd been here she'd already cut a swath through the unattached men on the island.

Sheer, savage rage fountained through Blair. Tamping it back down, she looked away, her decision to have nothing more to do with Hugh hardening. He'd kept his distance from her easily enough, but he was completely relaxed with Fiona Trickett. Because she was rich? If that was so then he was nothing but a snob. Blair's work as a decorator had introduced her to more than a few snobs, and almost without exception she had found them to be insecure, self-absorbed creatures. She felt sorry for them.

But she couldn't feel sorry for Hugh. What she felt was betrayal, raw and simple, as painful as a lash to her soul. It was easier to stigmatise him a snob than admit that he might be attracted to Fiona. Swinging on her heel, Blair walked out into the friendly night, trying to calm the furious torrent of her emotions.

The light fishers were working the lagoon, fashioning a net of gold across the dark waters, tying up creation in their nooses, each interstice punctuated with a pure golden bead of light. Enchanted, Blair lost herself in the sight, trying to file away details. Excitement ran down her spine, lifted her heart, tingled in her fingers. She watched with held breath as they wove their patterns on the unseen face of the sea.

But her mind couldn't leave the subject of Hugh Bannatyne and his treachery. Why had she reacted so strongly to that easy exchange of smiles?

Because nothing so simple had happened with her. Right from the start he had so obviously kept his distance. He hadn't wanted to smile at her, he'd despised himself for wanting her, and he despised her too, for her eager response.

So intent was she on her thoughts that the voices didn't impinge until they were too close for her to leave without being seen. Now, as she registered they were there, she also realised they had been talking for quite some time. One she recognised—Hugh. Her heart froze. But the other was unknown to her, a light, breathless young voice.

'. . . so I thought I'd ask you first. Do you think Gina would like it?'

Hugh's beautiful voice was grave. 'Yes, I think she probably would.'

The young voice was troubled. 'It's hard to know what to choose for her.' And then, with a confusion that Blair remembered only too well from her own adolescence, she added, 'Of course, it makes it much more of a challenge to buy her presents.'

'It does, but you seem to have a talent for choosing just the right gift. Gina always likes the things you get.'

He meant it, too. Obviously thrilled, his companion said, 'Well, I do try hard.'

Who was Gina? Clearly only an acquaintance, Blair decided, angry with herself for listening, and even angrier because for a moment she had been jealous. There had been no emotion in Hugh's voice when he had said the name.

She now knew who was with him—the Chapmans' older daughter Louise, a piquantly attractive girl of thirteen.

'Are you going to stay long?' Louise asked, trying to sound worldly and only too clearly revealing her thoughts. In her tone was all the shy adoration of first love.

‘No, not this time.’ With a note Blair had never heard in his voice before, a note of affection, of teasing almost, Hugh continued, ‘But we’ll be seeing you quite soon, anyway, when you go back to school. You’ll be coming to stay on your weekends of home leave, won’t you? You know Mrs Hastie loves feeding you up.’

‘Yes, of course I’m coming, except for the weekends when I stay with Gran and Grandad.’ Louise’s voice altered, to disclose the child behind the adult little façade. ‘Mrs Hastie is the best cook in the world. I just adore her pancakes and blueberries!’

‘Well, that’s settled, then. Let’s go in, and if you think your reputation can stand being seen with someone as old as I am we’ll dance this one out.’

‘Oh, Uncle Hugh, you’re not old.’

The hero-worship was so plain in her voice that Blair’s smile was tinged with wistfulness.

‘Almost as old as your father.’ His voice was amused, and he said something Blair couldn’t catch. Louise burst out laughing.

Five minutes later when she walked back through the doors she saw them dancing. Louise’s sparkling little face with its vaguely Gallic features revealed transparently that she was in seventh heaven. Hugh was obviously very fond of her. Perhaps, Blair thought painfully as Sam came up and slung a friendly arm over her shoulders, perhaps he could only let down his guard to those who were no threat to him.

She smiled up at Sam, and looked away again, to meet Hugh’s gaze. The cool, sexual appraisal in his eyes almost made her cry out in pain; she tightened her lips and lowered her lashes, turning her back on him.

‘Where have you been?’ Sam asked, drawing her into a group.

She managed to smile. 'Watching the light fishers. It's the most magical sight. I'm going to paint them, if I can possibly do it.'

Grant Chapman looked up. 'If you do,' he said, 'I'd like to see it.'

She nodded. 'Yes, of course.'

The Chapmans gave good parties. The people were an amalgam of locals and visitors; all had something to say and said it well, and the setting was superb, with the soft, scented darkness of the night working its subtle, subliminal magic on the most hardened cynics. The Japanese businessmen seemed to be enjoying themselves, too; Blair had a fascinating discussion about painted silk screens with one of them, and listened while another told her the basic tenets of Japanese landscape gardening.

Resolutely she did her bit to make the occasion swing. She smiled, she talked about a variety of subjects, some of them interesting, some not, she flirted mildly with the occasional man, she chatted with a couple of women, and wherever she was she made sure that Sam was not too far away. Indeed, for most of the evening he and she were together.

He hid his surprise well; he had, after all, only offered her a lift there and back, with no strings, but he followed her lead. Blair hoped that to anyone who was interested—and quite a few were, since Fala'isi was like a small town when it came to gossip—they seemed more than just friendly acquaintances.

That night, however, most of the locals' attention was fixed on one particular flirtation, and the onlookers' concern was more censorious than friendly. Both the participants were married, but not to each other, and they were not being discreet at all.

'Playing with fire,' Sandy MacDonald said forthrightly. 'Stupid idiots. Douglas Gardner won't like this when he hears about it, and he will—somebody's bound to tell him that Marya has been giving Neil Brown a lot more than a few come-hither looks.'

Blair sipped her glass of wine. The woman with Sandy said uncomfortably, 'It's just a flirtation. Look at Pauline; she doesn't seem to mind.'

'Pauline is absolutely furious,' Sandy said grimly, 'but she's too clever to cause a scene, especially here. Would you throw a tantrum here, Lina, whatever the provocation?'

'Well, no, I suppose not,' Lina admitted. 'The Chapmans would never invite you back.'

The three women watched as Neil bent over and whispered something into Marya's ear. It was perfectly obvious to even the most uninterested observer that he finished by giving the lobe a seductive little nip.

Lina gasped. 'What on earth does Neil think he's playing at?'

'Some men,' Blair said, her voice icy with disdain, 'can't help it. They think with their gonads, not their heads, or their hearts. It looks as though Neil Brown is one of them. He's flattered, and when Marya flutters her lashes he can't see past the end of them.'

'Come on, it's not his fault entirely,' Lina pointed out in an attempt to be fair. 'What about Marya? I mean, she's not exactly making it hard for him, is she? You'd think she'd have some sort of loyalty to her husband.'

Sandy shrugged. 'A couple of weeks ago Marya told me in strictest confidence a very spicy bit of gossip she'd been told—also in the strictest confidence.'

Lina looked startled, and then embarrassed. Blair hoped that she wasn't the one Marya had betrayed. To hide the awkward moment she said calmly, 'She's not loyal to her friends, so why should she be loyal to her husband? Fidelity isn't solely sexual.'

Sandy sent her a knowledgeable glance, a glance that altered somewhere in the region of Blair's shoulder. 'Oh, hello, Mr Bannatyne,' she said cheerfully. 'We're just discussing loyalty. Blair's all for it. How about you?'

For some reason Blair's breath caught in her throat as she waited for his answer. When it came, it was in a voice completely emptied of emotion. 'Like Blair, I'm all for it. At least until the object of the loyalty turns out to be not worthy of it. Then it's self-defeating and counter-productive.'

There was a moment's silence until Sandy grinned. 'I rather think that might be the last word on loyalty. Can't you stay away from Fala'isi, Mr Bannatyne? It's not that long since you were here last time.'

'My name is Hugh,' he said easily. 'And I like the island. I call in as often as I can.'

Ten minutes later Blair had to admit that watching him like this was a revelation. A smooth charm she hadn't seen before reeled the other two women in like willing fish. He had them eating out of his hand.

Not by word or intonation, not by look or gesture, did he reveal that he and Blair were anything more to each other than the slightest of acquaintances. She should have been relieved. Instead, she was obscurely, bitterly disappointed, a response which made her furious with herself. As soon as she could, she made an excuse and rejoined Sam.

She took good care not to look in Hugh's direction for the rest of the night.

Much later, when they left, as Sam handed her into the car with a flourish that owed much to the very good whisky he had been drinking, she felt the hair on the back of her neck lift in a primitive reaction to danger. Very slowly, she turned her head a fraction, and saw Hugh watching her from the shadows of the pillared entrance.

Sam drove painstakingly home, and because she knew he wouldn't take advantage of it she asked him in for coffee. On the way he had been talking once more about his children, about his fears that they were growing away from him. Blair felt sorry for him. Men, she knew, rarely had male friends who were prepared to act as sounding-boards. They relied on women to do that for them.

So she made coffee and listened sympathetically, putting in the odd word now and then but mostly letting him talk it out.

On the third cup he sighed. 'Why don't you tell me to take my troubles home and deal with them myself?'

'You are dealing with them.'

'How? By inflicting my woes on you?'

She shook her head. 'You're not inflicting them on me, you're talking them through. However broad your shoulders are it always helps to talk to someone with an objective outlook. Why do you men feel you have to cope with everything by yourself? It's not a weakness to need to discuss problems with someone else, you know.'

'Our conditioning, I suppose. You know, when we grew up men were supposed to be the strong ones. Our fathers taught us that women were to be protected and sheltered from the harsh facts of life.' His grin was self-derisory. 'They did us a great disservice. My own daughter is tougher than I am, and she's only eight.'

Blair laughed, but said, 'Really strong men can admit to being vulnerable.'

'Not when it comes to divorce,' he countered acidly. 'Narelle took me for everything she could, and she knew damned well I'd let her get away with it because the kids are my weakness and she has custody. I even gave her that without a fight; a hotel's no place to bring kids up on your own. It doesn't pay to expose yourself, Blair; you have to act tough, otherwise you're taken to the cleaners.'

'The law of the jungle?' she scoffed.

'Yeah.' He got to his feet, smiling with such cynicism that she felt sorry for him. 'That's life. Show that you can be screwed, and you'll get screwed.'

'Yet you're probably one of the kindest men I've ever met. So your cynical philosophy doesn't hold water.'

He shrugged, made uneasy by her frankness. 'Anything I've done for you has been good business,' he said offhandedly. 'Your paintings sell, and your presence is always welcome. Men like beautiful women!'

She laughed again, but didn't press the point. At the doorway he bent and kissed her lightly on the mouth. 'Thanks,' he said, and strode off to the car.

Blair waited until the red glow of the rear lights winked out, then turned back into the house. Exhaustion ached through her; not just end-of-day weariness, although she was surprised to realise that Sam had been talking for almost two hours, but a bone-deep tiredness that sleep wouldn't relieve.

Blast Hugh Bannatyne! She could actually taste the need and hunger that kept her awake at night. Sometimes she woke with his scent in her nostrils, the feel of his sleek skin on her fingertips.

Yet it was more than a simple physical urge. Why did she miss him so much, miss his conversation, his swift, penetrating logic, the powerful intellect that stretched her own mind? The initial bonding had happened before they'd made love. The physical union, although mind-blowing, had merely reinforced the intangible links between them.

Was it love? As she lay in her bed, the sounds of the waves on the reef filling her brain, Blair tried to understand just what it was that she felt for him. No, it couldn't be love. Love was based on mutual interests, on sharing. She and Hugh had nothing in common. He was too aloof, too withdrawn to be understood, and although he had wanted her—still wanted her—she understood his resentment at the strength of that sensual pull. His independence, his freedom from the burden of emotions, was too important to him.

Something incredibly traumatic must have happened in his past, something horrendous, if the only way he could survive such feelings was to block them off.

Probably in his childhood, she thought. That was when the most painful traumas were formed. She wondered what he had looked like as a child. Had those strong features been softened by youth, or had he always been angular and decisive?

Beneath his arrogant composure there burned a heat that called to something as intense in her, something fierce and unregenerately primitive. She had been attracted to it from the start, like a moth drawn to destruction by a flame.

Blair was frowning when she finally drifted off to sleep, and woke the next morning with a headache. After eating a slice of chilled pineapple and two cups of coffee she went into the studio, but she couldn't settle. Half an hour later she gave up and changed into a bikini. Perhaps a swim would clear her head and get her going.

As usual the beach was empty, the sand lapped by water gleaming like a promise of heaven. She walked slowly into water as smooth and as clinging as silk, enjoying the rippling tug of the current against her skin. For once she didn't swim, just lay on her back, occasionally turning over to look at the sandy bottom with its outcroppings of coral heads and tiny, brilliant fish.

Although she had slathered herself with sunblock she didn't stay in the water for more than twenty minutes or so. She had slept late and the sun was getting too high in the sky to be comfortable, even in the water. Feeling oddly lethargic and heavy, she paddled back to the shore and stood up, pushing her hair back from her face.

The balustrade seemed to be an enormous distance away. Sighing, she walked across the glittering white sand, up the steps and along the side of the house to the terrace where the pool, shaded beneath a creeper-covered pergola, gleamed its impossible blue. There had been a few instances of petty pilfering on the beach, and as a precaution she had left her clothes and towel on a chair beside the pool, safely out of sight.

She was almost halfway across the flagstones when Hugh came around the corner of the house. Incredulous, Blair stared at him. He stopped beneath the creeper's green canopy, right beside the chair that held her clothes and towel. He looked grimly furious, a deeper shadow in the shade. Blair froze in instant reaction to the scathing flick of his glance, cuttingly scornful, yet lit from within by cold appreciation.

Her mouth tightening, she forced herself to go towards him, refusing to let him see how startled she was.

'What do you want?' she said with as much poise as she could muster.

He watched as she grabbed her towel from the back of the chair and shrugged it defensively around her shoulders. He didn't pick it up for her; in a man so naturally courteous the unusual little omission had an impact much greater than it would have with any other man.

'Why did you come back?' Blair asked imperiously.

His smile was mirthless, harsh with a savage irony. 'Because I couldn't stay away.'

Her head straight and high, she willed her tone, her stance to shout her rejection. 'Go back to New Zealand, Hugh.'

'Why?'

'I don't want you, I certainly don't need you.'

His hand on her shoulder was a stark statement of possession. 'No?' he drawled, bringing her around and against him in one swift, sure movement. His eyes glittered as though he had a fever. 'When we made love did I arouse needs you had forgotten?' he said, watching her still, proud face with the unnerving patience of a hunter. 'Because you hadn't slept with a man for quite a long time, had you? Is that why you took the manager of the hotel into your bed last night?'

White-faced, Blair gasped, her furious indignation warring with caution. Indignation won. 'I did not sleep with Sam last night!'

'No?'

She read his disbelief in a gaze as cold and turbulent as a winter storm, in the twist to his lips, in the assessing look that flicked down her body. Her temper began to build. Through her teeth she said, 'No, I did not, you arrogant swine. How the hell did you know he was here?'

'Does it matter?' he asked contemptuously. 'I know he stayed with you for a couple of hours last night, and I'm damned sure you didn't just spend the time talking. You're a passionate woman, with strong needs and a direct way of satisfying them, and he's made no secret of the fact that he wants you. From the way you were flirting with him at the Chapmans' you had every intention of going to bed with him.'

'I did not go to bed with him,' she ground out. It was vitally important that he should accept this.

With weary resignation she saw him reimpose control, watching the inner struggle with an anger that was only half directed at him. After a moment he searched her face with newly impassive eyes, so densely opaque that no emotions shone through. Then he said quietly, 'All right, I believe you.'

'Even if I did,' she retorted through stiff lips, 'you have no right to expect me to offer you the same service.'

His smile was pure, unadulterated intimidation. 'Why not? You want me.'

Of course he could tell; he was an experienced man. He knew what the dilation of her pupils, the sudden quiver in her voice, the dew across her temples meant. He was fully attuned to the subtle, significant signals that indicated a woman's readiness, her need.

'You want me,' he repeated inexorably, 'just as much as I want you. You've spent nights lying in an empty bed with the sheets tangled around you, haven't you, remembering what it was like when we made love? That primal need still echoes through you, and the wild tremors, the helpless arch of your body is imprinted in your cells. Don't even try to lie, Blair, because I know. I've been there.'

Desire clutched at her body, honey-sweet and heavy, slowing her brain, readying her in a thousand subliminal ways. Touching her tongue to dry lips, she winced at the tiny flares of light in his eyes, and said desperately, 'All right, so I might want you, but that doesn't mean I have to let you—I'm not an animal with no will-power. I don't want to feel like this.'

'Neither do I.' There was no mistaking the ring of truth in the words, or the hard sombreness that showed for a moment in the uncompromising lines of his face. 'But for once in my life it seems that I'm going to have to cope with a feeling I can't control.'

'You can't just rape me!' Real panic flared into her voice, rendering it shrill.

His brows shot up. He fixed her with a glance that pierced its way right down into her frightened soul.

'No,' he said through barely moving lips, 'I won't rape you. I'm not some pervert who gets his kicks from terrorising women.' As though gentling a small wild animal, his beautiful voice dropped several notes. 'I want you,' he said reasonably, 'and you want me. What's so wrong about that? We were perfect together, weren't we, as smoothly fitting as a hand and its glove? All I want is to enjoy your warmth and your passion and your fire some more. Blair——'

He kissed her, and, forgetting everything, she opened her mouth for him. She ached for him with a slow, intoxicating drumming of need that was as seductive as his voice, his mouth, the measured caress of his hands across her back. But a last, rear-guard instinct of self-preservation whipped her into action.

Dragging herself free, she said, 'Very well,' forcing the words out.

She stepped back and wrenched off the towel and her bikini-top, watching with a flat, scornful gaze as his eyes darkened at the sight of her breasts, which were sleek and gleaming with the sheen of water.

'What would you like me to do?' she asked thinly, head held high. 'I've been trained to make love in all sorts of ways, I can do whatever you like, however you like; I can make it so good for you that you'll never forget, you'll never be able to sleep with another woman without remembering me. Is that what you want?'

She had shocked him, but although his eyes widened almost immediately they were hidden again by his lashes. 'Trained?' he said, and then, with a sudden icy control, 'Were you a courtesan, Blair?'

'Does it matter?' She was already regretting her impetuous words.

Smiling bitterly, he drew her close to him and bent his head to kiss under her jaw, to bite the lobe of her ear. 'No,' he muttered, his voice setting off tiny internal shivers through her, 'it doesn't matter in the least. Show me how you make love, Blair. Last time was a whirlwind, a moment out of time. This time, and every other time from now on, make it long and slow and hot, burning me up, burning you up...'

She shivered, struggling, desperate. 'You make it sound as though you want some sort of relationship.'

His head lifted. 'Is there any reason why that can't happen? Is there someone else?'

'No, there's no one else.' Chills were pulling her skin tight. She blurted out the truth. 'But I'm—I'm not ready for any sort of commitment.'

I'm afraid, she could have said; every love-affair I've ever had has gone wrong, and this one will too. And that thought terrifies me, because I think this would hurt the most; this would be such pain that I couldn't cope with it.

But she didn't say any of that.

He hesitated, before saying quietly, 'All right, then, no commitment. I know how you feel about your independence. I certainly don't want to interfere with that, or with your work. I admire it very much, and even if I didn't know it is the most important thing in your life I wouldn't expect you to make compromises for me. But I want you; I want to warm my cold heart in your warmth, that golden aura that glows around you. I can't forget that miraculous night we spent together.'

Miraculous was a strange word to use, but it had been miraculous for her too, the sundering of chains she had been wearing for almost three long years.

Blair wanted to surrender, so much. An icy shudder forced its way up inside her. She looked at him, at the face which was etched on to her brain cells, at the big, lean, huntsman's body which had taken her to a paradise she hadn't even known existed. Was she in love with him? She didn't know; she only knew that she had never felt like this before. If any other man had offered her what he was offering her—a long-distance affair—she would have told him to get the hell out of her life.

But she couldn't, and somehow that was the greatest betrayal of all, for the treachery was her own, against herself.

She said harshly, 'I should tell you to go.'

He smiled, seeing past her self-command, her poise, to the woman who wanted him, who had lain dreaming of him night after night in her empty bed. Deliberately he let his gaze wander down, coming to rest on her breasts, suddenly heavy now and with nipples that were hardening into small, provocative peach nubs, giving away exactly how that assessing glance affected her.

Blair wanted to fight, she wanted to throw his cheap desire back in his face, but when she looked at him she saw nothing but naked, haunted hunger revealed in his eyes, in the strong, severe lines of his face. For the first time ever he had lowered his guard, and she wasn't proof against that. She supposed it was passion, this wild hunger, this cell-deep need for another. Certainly she had never experienced anything like it before, but that moment when he was exposed to her sealed her fate. Just for a second she closed her eyes in despair, then she yielded.

'But you're not going to,' he said confidently, and without touching her he bent his head and kissed her breasts, lightly, gently, until the fountain of fire inside her reached the skin, and she swayed. Then his mouth became more insistent.

'No,' she whispered. 'Not here.'

'No.' His voice shook as he took her hand and led her into the house. 'Not out here.'

It was nothing like the first time. That had been fire and flame, the unambiguous sating of a famished need. This was subtle, the slide of fingers over skin, the leisurely removal of clothes until they were both naked, the tremble of his hand as he cupped her breasts, pushing them up to his avid mouth. Blair was shivering. Her innermost part, the area of her that had been hitherto inviolate, lay bared to him, because she could no longer protect herself from her own emotions.

'Golden woman,' he said huskily, 'like a sun maiden——'

'I'm no maiden.'

His smile against her breasts was slow and sensuous. 'I don't want to initiate a virgin. I want a woman in my arms, in my bed, a woman with a woman's needs and a woman's appetites. I don't want to teach, I want an equal.'

When he picked her up she gasped and flung her arms about his neck. He lifted her, the muscles in his arms bulging against her back and legs, and without any alteration to his breathing carried her into the bedroom, finding his way unerringly. It gave her a purely atavistic thrill to be carried like a precious burden.

His size, his strength made her feel small and protected, yet completely in his power. But she wasn't; she had experienced helplessness in El Amir, and that had only made her sick with fear and outrage. She looked up at the jutting line of Hugh's jaw, and then down at the smooth globes of her breasts, naked against his fine cotton shirt.

How had she dared to strip off her top? Had it been a secret plea, an indication by her unconscious that she was ready for him, that in spite of the logical and sensible reasons why they shouldn't get together she wanted him?

He slid her down his body, holding her hips against his so that she felt his need and the stark male power of arousal—— And remembered something she should have thought before.

'Hugh!' she exclaimed. 'I can't, not now. I don't want to get pregnant——'

A smile of consummate irony curled his mouth. 'Will you think I'm the arrogant swine you called me if I tell you I can deal with that?'

Her mouth compressed, but she said lightly, 'Were you so confident of winning?'

'There's no winning or losing in this, between us, and no. I just wanted to make sure that if the occasion arose I was prepared.'

She might have said something else, but he kissed her, and everything but his mouth, and the warm, sun-scented tang of him, fled from her mind. She clutched the solid muscle of his upper arms, leaning into the kiss, her body curving into a taut bow before relaxing against his. His hands settled around her waist, the lean fingers biting into the soft flesh there, then easing upwards.

Blair held her breath as he lifted his head and looked down. A swift movement of his hands rendered her breasts luscious, forbidden fruit in his palms.

'You taste of paradise,' he said deeply. 'Of warmth and woman, your own particular scent and taste, as sweet and as erotic as a summer night.'

His words stirred something deep inside her, something that had never been touched before. Like ripples across a pool it spread through her body, fire and water combined, sharp as alcohol, a tang in her blood that set sensation roaring along her nerves.

His voice deepened, the beautiful timbre thickening into urgency. 'And you feel like the petals of a sun-kissed flower, silky and living and vibrant, warm with life and passion, with kindness and laughter.'

He kissed her eyes shut, then his mouth lingered over the smooth cream column of her throat, until he smiled against her skin and murmured, 'Much as I like this, I think we'd be more comfortable lying on the bed.'

He released her, and for a moment she stood looking at him, wondering why she should feel so—*virginal*. She had been married to Gerald for five years, she had made impassioned love with Hugh, yet she could feel heat rising through her skin, and she knew she just didn't have it in her to take off the tight bottom half of her bikini with him watching.

'Blair!' he said, his eyes glinting with satisfaction. 'You're shy!'

She held his gaze, even though her skin felt scorched. 'Stupid, isn't it?' she agreed, trying to salvage some sort of sophistication.

He laughed softly. 'Endearing, rather.' He pulled his shirt over his head and dropped it, saying calmly, 'Now we're equal. Why don't you undress me while I try to get those off? That way neither of us will be embarrassed.'

It was difficult, because they kept getting in each other's way, and it wasn't made any easier by the fact that Blair started to laugh helplessly, but at last she managed to slide his trousers down, and then step out of her bikini-bottoms. Instead of pushing her on to the bed he dropped to his knees in front of her and said quietly, 'I've dreamed of this.'

His mouth on the fine skin at her waist was heated and demanding. Blair looked down at the dark head, the way his hair grew across it, and her heart swelled. Desire and passion she understood, but this was totally new to her. She had fallen in love with Hugh Bannatyne, and she would love him until the end of her life. Sudden tears blurred her vision; she lifted a hand and ran it through the clinging auburn silk of his hair, cupping the hard line of his cheek as he turned his face into her stomach. The words trembled on her tongue, but she swallowed them.

Love had no place in their arrangement. He wanted her, but he hadn't mentioned anything about loving.

He kissed her navel, his tongue searching out the tiny indentation. Such an intimate touch sent quivers through her, until her knees buckled and she said huskily, 'I'm going to collapse.'

He laughed, and got to his feet and kissed her mouth, and her throat, and the junction of neck and shoulder, biting it gently, letting her feel his undisguised passion. Jagged splinters of sensation lodged in her bloodstream, stopping her breath in her throat, reducing her to a strange languor. His mouth crushing hers again, he picked her up and carried her across to the bed.

This time their movements were unhurried; locked in the grip of a lassitude unlike anything Blair had ever experienced, she thought it was like seeing a film in slow motion, the way his hand stroked her skin, the powerful thud of her heart in her breast, her boneless lack of energy as she ran her fingers through his hair and curled her hand around his neck, feeling his life-force pulse against it, the strong sinews and tendons, the surging masculine virility. Her eyelids were weighted with anticipation.

He kissed her as though he had searched the world for her, as though she was more precious to him than life itself, and he didn't stop at her mouth. His touch sent fire through her; her breath lodged in her throat when he kissed her breasts. Instinctively she held his head a long moment there, feeling the jutting line of his cheekbone against her soft flesh. The tight peach aureoles peaked, demanding, supplicating, and at last, when her whole body was strung tight, he enclosed one in his avid, tender mouth, suckling strongly.

Fire fountained through her, turning her bones to liquid, sweet as honey, harsh as hunger. In a quick, involuntary movement her hips pushed against him; she felt his response, growing, urgent, but instead of taking her he said thickly, 'No, not yet, not yet.'

'I want you.'

He smiled down at her importunate, imperious face. 'Not, my heart, as much as you are going to. Last time was too quick, too greedy. This time we've got all the time in the world, and we are going to take it. I want to pleasure you properly, as a lover should.'

She protested, but he pushed her a little sideways and kissed the other breast. Gritting her teeth, she said, 'Damn you, Hugh!'

He looked up, his eyes gleaming. 'Why?'

'I want you now!'

But he laughed, the sound oddly significant in the quiet bedroom. 'No, not yet.'

Was he going to make her beg? She was already unbearably stimulated, ready for him, her body aching with the need to enfold him, take him within her, feel the urgent thrusts of his body against hers.

'Touch me,' he said.

CHAPTER FIVE

DRAWING a long, sobbing breath, Blair put her hand up to his shoulder, surprised to feel the muscles bunch and quiver beneath her fingers. His skin was hot; she could smell the scent of his arousal, male, incredibly stimulating.

Two, she thought hazily, could play at his game. Slowly she ran her hand across his back, down the sleekness of his spine, and over the taut muscles of his backside.

He said huskily, 'Yes, touch me like that.'

Blair didn't need the encouragement; she was intent on exploring. Beneath the pattern of hair his chest was satin-smooth, and when she tried to span his midriff with her hands it was with a growing excitement, for he wasn't trying to hide what her leisurely caresses were doing to him.

Smouldering blue irises were almost swallowed by the darkness of each pupil, and the skin had tightened over the angular framework of his face, chiselling it with hunger into a mask of primal desire, almost cruel with need.

Blair kissed his shoulder, then bit it, and licked the small red crescent she had made. From the corners of her eyes she noted his reaction, the hard smile, the way his eyes gleamed. He pushed her breast up, and bent to suckle again, this time not worrying about gentleness. A primitive flower of sensuality unfolded inside her; pleasure penetrated every cell. Again her hips jerked, and her hand slid down, met the steel-smooth length of his masculine member.

'No,' he said in a strangled voice, his big body clenching.

Wild as an enchantress, Blair laughed, a smoky, seductive sound, before bending her head to flick a wet kiss across each small male nipple; she pressed herself against him with sinuous determination, until he groaned something deep and shaken in his throat and rolled over her, filling her with one hard thrust as though his life depended on it.

Even then, although sweat beaded his face and his features were made almost haggard by feral craving, he forced himself to hold back. 'Damn you,' he said savagely. 'I wanted to make this slow and easy, give you that, at least.'

Stabbed by hunger, she ran her hands once more down his back before pulling his hips towards her. 'I need you,' she said through soft red lips, taking him in further and further in a movement she had learned from two women in a small mud fort half a world away. Her inner muscles gripped then relaxed, tightened and loosened.

The wildness in his face overcame the ferocious control he had imposed on himself. 'On your own head, then.'

'On my own head.'

It was like making love with a storm, a whirlwind. Hugh was fierce and masterful, demanding everything, not giving any quarter. Such was the fury of his lovemaking that Blair knew she would have bruises, yet she responded with an equal violence, losing at long last the constraints of civilisation and fear, losing herself in the act of love with a participation that went beyond willingness to become insistence.

She fought him for domination, only yielding when the climax overtook her. Her body bent upwards like a strung bow. She cried out as the waves of ecstasy flowed through her, carrying her further and faster than any ever before, rocketing her into some sort of timeless space where all that she understood was the rapture that shook her. Instantaneously he followed, racked by the same flood of sensation.

When it was over she was exhausted, replete as never before. Hugh collapsed on to her, but almost immediately stirred and began to lift himself off.

'No,' she murmured, the word blurred. Her arms tightened across his back.

'I'm too heavy.'

Her laughter was a breath of sound across his shoulder. 'You're perfect. Stay there.'

He did, but after a few minutes he moved and scooped her to lie across him, her head on his shoulder. With a smile on her lips and his scent filling her nostrils, Blair slept.

When she awoke she stretched, wondering for an astounded second just what had happened. Her eyes fixed on to white curtains drifting on the soft sea breeze; she frowned, then realisation roared back into her brain in an overwhelming flood of memory, and she stiffened.

'No,' Hugh said harshly, reaching across to keep her beside him. 'Second thoughts are rarely the best ones. The decision is made, and it's no use worrying about it now.'

'As easy as that?'

He smiled, but there was no amusement in his expression. 'It hasn't been easy for me,' he said. 'Was it so easy for you?'

'No,' she said on a sigh.

He lifted her chin. The dazzling blue of his eyes held her captive, drowning her. 'But this,' he said quietly, 'this is very easy. I meant what I said before. I can't get you out of my mind, but I don't want to complicate your life. I'll come whenever I can, and be faithful to you when I'm not here.'

Blair would have followed him around the world, but she sensed that he didn't want such a sacrifice from her. In spite of the heated passion of his lovemaking he was still a man who needed space, a man to whom control was as necessary as breathing. Some day, she vowed, he would discover that when he was with her he didn't need to keep behind those barricades, but it was too early for him to trust her yet.

Her smile was bitter-sweet. 'Yes, all right.'

He drew her closely against him and bent his head, his mouth as searching as his eyes. Relaxing, her body afire with expectation, she let him lead her down into dark, all-consuming oblivion.

She thought he would go back to the hotel, so it gave her a quiet *frisson* of pleasure when he asked if he could move in with her. It was strange to be living with a man again. She thought he might become angry when she went into the studio each morning, but he spent much of his day working at what seemed dry-as-dust papers. By unspoken consent they never spoke of his life in New Zealand, or his work. Instead they discussed the world, art and music and travel, the books they had read, their opinions on a thousand subjects. He proved to her that her cynicism about politics and politicians was almost as dangerous as being corrupt, and she teased him unmercifully for what she called his right-wing views.

They had almost nothing in common, yet he was the most interesting, fascinating man she had met. Blair loved matching wits with him, she liked to watch the gleam of humour in his blue eyes as he politely contradicted her, she found herself being deliberately outrageous for the pleasure of arguing with him. She had never met a man who suited her so well.

She loved him.

She was more than content to stay at home, and it seemed that he was, too, for he never suggested they go out.

'You have such a lazy laugh,' he said one afternoon, ten days after he had moved in with her. Their discussion on the conservation movement had somehow been side-tracked, and they were now sprawled out on the big bed. Through the shutters the sea dazzled her eyes. It was quiet except for the muted thunder of the rollers, small, slow swells today, just smoothing their way on to the reef.

'Lazy?'

'Mmm. Lazy, and sensual, and provocative. You laugh the way Helen of Troy probably did, with such promise of passion, such husky light-heartedness—I heard you laugh before I saw you surrounded by men, and I wanted you from that moment on.'

Blair rolled over, looking into his face. Sated passion had slackened the rigid control, the shuttered, guarded look she had noticed at first, but his defences were still palpably in place. He made love to her with the untamed ferocity of a barbarian of old, yet when it was over the walls were unbreached. It hurt, because more than anything else now she wanted to be invited in to his guarded heart, to become part of his life, not just an adjunct.

'The first thing I noticed about you,' she said, watching him from beneath heavy eyelids, 'was that you were tall and exciting, and you had a face that would make poker players green with envy.'

Something moved in the depths of his eyes. 'Really? And here I've been hoping that it was my stunning good looks you fell for.'

She grinned. 'You looked like some grim god, terrifying yet infinitely interesting. I couldn't get you out of my mind.'

'Nor I you.' His hand cupped a breast, idly measuring the soft, heavy curve of it. 'And when I saw you, golden and gleaming, with that seductive swaying walk, never hurrying, taking your time, my whole body tightened. It's like a madness. Has it ever happened to you before?'

Blair sent him a swift look. She could read nothing from his face, but her heart beat a little faster. Was this the beginning of true understanding? Was he going to open up emotionally? 'No,' she said quietly. 'Never before.'

'Not for me, either. Nothing like it. I thought people who looked at each other and were hit by lightning were deluding themselves. Serves me right for being so arrogant, I suppose.'

'Do you regret it?'

His mouth stretched into a sardonic smile. 'No. I don't like being at the mercy of my hormones, but, provided you're at the mercy of yours as well, the way we make love is enough to stop me from regretting anything.'

Blair closed her eyes to hide the sudden, painful shadows in them. She had been stupid to press. What had made him so wary, so distrustful of himself and of love that he couldn't see their affair as being anything more than a mutual satisfaction of need?

Well, she had had her own demons, and she hadn't told him about them. In time he would learn to trust her.

'What's the matter?' he asked her, confounding her once again by his ability to read her mind.

She stretched, revelling in the heated hunger of his gaze as he watched her skin flex and her body undulate.

'I must be tired,' she said, smiling at him, banishing the hurt.

It was obvious he didn't believe her; he sent her a quick, sharp glance. But clearly this was as far as he intended to take this subject, for he brushed her breasts with a slow, suggestive hand. 'Pity,' he said lightly, watching her helpless reaction with glinting eyes. 'I'm not tired in the least.'

With clenched jaw Blair endured the light stroking, willing her body not to reveal any of her scorching reaction. He knew her so well, knew exactly what to do to shatter the walls of her control. But then, she knew him, too. If she lifted her head and very gently grazed the small masculine nipple with her teeth he would shudder with pleasure.

'I have to go on Wednesday,' he said abruptly.

Blair's face grew still and blank. 'I see.'

'Will you be here when I come back?'

She bit her lip. 'I—yes. Yes, I'll be here.' And before she could stop herself she said, 'When will that be?'

'As soon as I can,' he said quietly. 'In a couple of months, probably.' And his mouth on her throat worked the magic that drew them both down into a vortex of sensuality.

He didn't want her to see him off on the plane, so they said their farewells at the house and he left without looking back. With him went the pictures he had bought the first time he was there.

Blair threw herself into an orgy of painting; it helped, although these paintings were too personal to sell or exhibit. She spent her days ripping out her heart to display on canvas.

It was the nights she found agonising. Every so often she would remind herself that she didn't know Hugh's address, that he might never return, and that even if he did it would only be to resume their affair. She had never suffered this aching incompletion, this lack of confidence before, and it outraged her.

Ten days after he'd left the letter came. The minute she saw it Blair knew who it was from; even if she hadn't seen his signature she would, she thought as excitement fountained through her, have recognised his writing. The angular black letters revealed his character, sharp and authoritative and disciplined, without any excess ornamentation.

Ripping open the envelope, she sank down on to a chair and read the letter. He had been called to Auckland for a particularly interesting case of international law, and was likely to be there for another week or so to get things going. He sketched in the case, without giving away anything more than she could have read in the newspapers, before giving dry, rather acidly humorous thumbnail sketches of the people involved.

He had seen *Chess*, which he'd enjoyed, and had been persuaded by friends to go with them when they took their small son to the zoo to see the meerkats. His descriptions of crawling along a tunnel so that the four-year-old could peer through a transparent dome at the animals, and the small mammals' reactions to this invasion, were funny. He was the only adult fit enough to do this; the child's mother was heavily pregnant and his father had a fear of enclosed spaces.

Me, too, Blair thought, but the momentary chill of panic was washed away by amusement. Sighing, she wished she'd been there with him, then returned to the letter. He told her of a book he'd read and thought she might like, commented on a well-known politician who had managed to make a fool of himself yet again, and ended hers, Hugh. No expression of affection, but then she hadn't really expected a letter. Unconsciously her eyes drifted to the address, a box number in Napier.

Her mouth twisted. Plenty of people used their box numbers as their addresses, so why did it seem like a slap in the teeth?

She was suffering, she decided, from that well-known syndrome, mistress's insecurity, and unless she could overcome it they weren't going to have a very happy relationship.

Smiling determinedly, she began an answer. She would treat Hugh just the same as she did her other correspondents, writing a letter in the form of a diary, with the occasional sketch to express what words couldn't.

Napier, a miniature art deco city dreaming beside the wide stretch of its bay, city of wineries and horticulture with the sweep of the ranges in the hinterland...

When she left Fala'isi, would he ask her to live in Napier with him?

'Stop it!' she commanded herself aloud, getting to her feet with a quick, angry movement. Why couldn't she enjoy what he was prepared to give her without demanding more? She had been sure that she would never be able to love again, never lose herself in physical ecstasy, yet it had happened. With Hugh she lost all thought, all concern. Surely that was enough for the moment?

But what was she to do about this inconvenient and difficult love?

Well, even though she had reached thirty, she told herself wryly, she was still attractive, and she thought that as well as wanting her he liked her. If he didn't he would learn to. And after liking came loving.

Ignoring the sly voice in her mind which told her that with Hugh nothing was so easy, she went into the studio and began work again.

He came back to Fala'isi six weeks later. The first Blair knew of it was when she emerged from the en suite bathroom at the tail end of a long, hot afternoon spent painting in the mountains, and found him sitting on the terrace watching the evening, long legs stretched out in front, his face drawn as though the intervening weeks had been difficult ones. He had flown up in a business suit; the jacket was slung over another chair, his discreet tie coiled on top of it. He had undone the top button of his shirt, and rolled back the sleeves to reveal muscular forearms, their copper skin lightly dusted with hair.

If she hadn't known how she felt about him before, Blair would have had it forcibly rammed home then. Her heart leapt like a hooked fish, then plunged down again, because she recognised tiredness and strain in the autocratic features and the bleak blue eyes. She couldn't, of course, do what she wanted to and fling herself on to his lap, but she was profoundly glad that she had showered off the paint and the smell of turpentine.

In a voice that was too even she said, 'Hugh, when did you get here?'

He looked up sharply, then got to his feet in a movement that was a little less than lithe. With an aching heart Blair saw him compose his face into the hard mask of impassivity.

'Twenty minutes ago.'

So he'd been in Australia, for the only plane that afternoon came from Melbourne. Fala'isi was certainly not on his way home. Something tight and wondering eased in Blair's throat. Without trying to hide her pleasure, she smiled at him. 'You should have told me you were here.'

His answering smile was tinged with mockery. 'You were in the shower, and I wanted to unwind first. Don't worry, I've been enjoying myself just sitting.'

'Then sit back down again and I'll get you a drink.'

But he came with her and poured himself a gin and lime, her a glass of cool, pale gold wine.

'Let's go back out on to the terrace,' she suggested, oddly ill at ease. 'It's my favourite way to end the day.'

He lifted his brows at her, but he went back out and together, unspeaking, they watched the sun go down and the darkness fall like a benediction over the island, thick and purple-blue, with the arch of heaven illuminated by stars so brilliant that it was like living in a bowl of diamonds.

'I wish I could paint that,' Blair said on a sigh.

His voice was amused yet rueful. 'Leave something for nature.'

She smiled. 'Only nature's able to do it. But it's utterly beautiful, isn't it?'

'Yes. Do you miss New Zealand at all?'

'Oh, there are lots of things I miss about home. Winter, for a start.' Wine slid, crisp and flower-flavoured, down her throat. 'And—well, it's home. My parents are there. Fala'isi is lovely, but I'm a New Zealander, and you know what they say about us—we always go home.'

'So you're a patriot.'

She laughed softly. 'Guilty.'

'When you leave here, will you be going back to Auckland?'

His voice was even and toneless, but Blair's pulse quickened. Of course it could have been—almost certainly was!—an idle question dropped into the warm air.

Her shoulders moved infinitesimally. She sipped more of the wine before saying, 'I don't know. I'm going to enjoy the time I have here, and make up my mind when I go back.'

She thought he nodded, but it was difficult to see. In the shadow of the terrace roof the darkness was almost absolute, although she could discern the white patch that was his shirt. The scent of frangipani mingled with the salt of the sea and the faint, tropical hint of decay that was always in the air.

'Grant Chapman told me he'd bought a picture you did of the light fishers,' he said. 'He's very pleased with it.'

She replied calmly, 'Good. It was a swine to do. I didn't want to sentimentalise, yet it was difficult not to turn out South Sea Islands cliché number thirty—*The Lagoon at Night*.' She saw his smile.

'But you succeeded,' he said blandly.

'I hope so.' She got to her feet. 'I wasn't expecting you, so I'd better make sure I have enough food in the house to give you dinner.'

He stood too. 'I don't give a damn about dinner,' he said with raw emphasis.

Blair gasped as he picked her up and took her through the wide doors into the bedroom. Once inside he lowered her down his aroused body and kissed her with a famished hunger that sent shudders of ecstasy through her.

She was glad that he hadn't rushed her straight to bed, but that first kiss left her in no doubt that it was good manners rather than lack of desire, and she responded with a fervour that startled her.

'I need you,' he said harshly. 'Get undressed while I close the doors and shutters.'

She had taken off her sundress and was bending to remove the small scrap of silk that was all she had on when he came up from behind and slid his hands around to hold her against him. It was strangely exciting to be held like that, a prisoner in his arms, almost naked while he was still fully dressed.

With eyes that were becoming accustomed to the dimness, Blair looked through the open door into the huge mirror in the bathroom. In it she could see her pale body almost dwarfed by his shadowy darkness, the well-cut shirt a blatant contrast to his tanned skin and face.

'You bring out the primitive in me.' His deep voice was thickened with emotion. 'I'd always thought any liaison between a man and a woman should be conducted with courtesy and finesse, but when I'm near you restraint goes flying out the window and I forget all about courtesy. And as for finesse——' he laughed oddly and bent his head to bite gently at the junction of her neck and shoulder '—I want to ravish you so thoroughly that between us we call down the moon and make this room all the world.'

'When you're in this room, it *is* all the world.' Streams of fiery stars were shooting through Blair's bloodstream, setting off conflagrations wherever they touched. Six weeks had sharpened her appetites, made her hungry for the ecstasy and the oblivion that were waiting for her. She turned, and as he kissed her eased the buttons on his shirt free, flexing her fingers through the warm tangle of hair while his knowing mouth wreaked enchantment on her senses.

Much later, sated, still lying on top of him where she had collapsed, she said faintly into his shoulder, 'Does anyone ever die of making love?'

Laughter lifted his chest. 'I don't think so.'

'I'm surprised.' Minutes passed. When her heartbeat had settled down she continued languidly, 'I suppose we'd better eat. When did you last have a meal?'

'About ten hours ago. A very formal lunch in Melbourne. I slept on the plane.'

She started to sit up, but his arm about her shoulders hardened. 'Stay there. I like feeling you on me. Unless you're starving.'

Her stomach chose that moment to reproach her, and he laughed softly and let her go, stretching as he yawned. 'On the other hand, I don't want you to be so weak that you can't function properly. Stay there and I'll rustle you up something.'

'You can cook?'

He scooped her on to the bed beside him and kissed the top of her head. 'Of course I can cook. I'm an expert at making omelettes. Everybody likes them and you can eat them any time of the day or night. Don't move.'

But she got up and showered and remade the bed and was brushing her hair when he came back with a tray which he set on the table in the window.

'I love your hair,' he said, coming across to run his hands through it. 'It's like sunshine and firelight mixed, the best of both worlds. Come and eat your supper.'

She had put on her robe. He looked down at the trousers he had pulled on as he left the bed and smiled. 'I'll get into something a little more conventional,' he said.

'Not unless you're uncomfortable. I like you the way you are now.'

He lifted his brows at her, but sat down without putting on a shirt. He'd been right to call himself an expert. The omelettes were rich, creamy, perfectly prepared concoctions filled with shrimps and avocado. A pot of coffee scented the air. Blair ate with delicate greed, but her eyes kept coming back to the naked torso of the man opposite her, the way the soft light of the lamp picked out gleaming, red-gold highlights in his skin, the clean male contours.

Mixed with the admiration of a woman in love was a pure delight in his physical beauty and form, the spare, sleek lines of him, the way the colours in his skin and hair and eyes contrasted and blended so magnificently.

'I feel,' he said without noticeable expression, 'as though I'm next on the menu.'

Wondering whether she had offended him, Blair searched his face. Although his emotions were firmly shielded, deep in his eyes a spark glimmered, blue as the hottest flame. Her mouth curved. Leaning forward, she picked up his hand and bit with sharp teeth at the base of his thumb, sensing the inner tightening the unexpected little caress caused. Laughter and provocation gleamed greenly in her narrowed eyes. 'Do you mind?' she asked demurely.

His smile was slow and enigmatic. 'Ask me in ten minutes' time.'

Blair woke the next morning stiff and a little sore, but happier than she had ever been before. Beside her Hugh still slept, stretched out on his back in an attitude of complete relaxation and taking up more than his share of the available space. In a way this consoled her; in spite of his great natural talent at lovemaking, and the refinements that only experience could produce, he was clearly unaccustomed to sharing a bed.

Moving cautiously, she lifted herself on to her elbow and surveyed him intently. Even in sleep the strong, austere lines of his face revealed no hint of softness. Blair thought rather sadly that whatever inflicted that mask of control on his features was still active when he slept. Yet there was a subtle difference. He had a very sensuous mouth, the bottom lip excitingly curved, the top one straight and autocratic, but during the day it was disciplined into unrevealing severity. Now it was fuller, almost relaxed.

And, although he had beautiful eyes, in the daytime it was the force and power of his expression that one noticed, not that his lashes were long and curly, and that his brows were not black but a very dark brown with a faint red sheen along them.

A thin sliver of blue between those lashes revealed that he had woken. Smiling, Blair leaned over to kiss him. 'Good morning,' she said. 'Did you sleep well?'

'Like a log,' he said huskily, and pulled her down so that he could kiss her properly.

She would have been more than happy to spend the rest of the day in bed with him, but he got up almost immediately. When he asked what she was planning to do that day, she told him of her expeditions into the mountains.

'It sounds just what I need,' he decided. 'I'll sleep under a palm tree while you work.'

She laughed. 'No palm trees, not up there. Coconut palms are married to the sea.'

'Any tree will do.'

An hour later saw them in the four-wheel-drive vehicle she'd hired from the hotel, bumping up a track that was about as far removed from the sealed road that ran around the island as anything could be. Blair was driving, and Hugh's face was set in lines of something perilously close to anger.

When she reached the end of the track he said curtly, 'I don't like you risking your life like this.'

'I know the road's not too good, but it's safe, and I'm a good driver.'

'Yes, you are, but safe is not the word I'd use to describe that road. I don't want you coming up here again.'

Blair looked at him. The sun summoned glints of auburn from his head, hinting at a temper held well in control but nevertheless fiery. She said quietly, 'I'm sorry about that, but I want to finish the painting I'm working on.'

'In other words, mind your own business.'

Blair bit her lip, but she couldn't give in. 'I'm afraid so,' she said, getting out of the jeep. Something compelled her to add, 'I'm a grown woman, Hugh, and I know the difference between confidence and foolhardiness. I don't take too kindly to orders.'

He came around and lifted out her gear. 'How about requests?'

It hurt to refuse him, but Blair was well aware that if she gave him his own way in this he would assume that he had a right to impose limitations on her life. He was a natural autocrat. She could not allow herself to become dependent on him, even alter her life for him in any but the most basic ways. So she said, 'I have to make up my own mind.'

He set the easel down and a bag next to it, then turned to pinion her by the upper arms. 'Would a plea do it, then?' he said.

Blair's eyes darkened. 'I can't imagine you pleading.'

'Where you're concerned,' he said roughly, 'I don't seem to have any pride left. I can't bear the thought of you wandering around these mountains and driving up goat tracks like the one we've just come up. Anything could happen. Stay off them, Blair, please.'

She almost agreed. She would have, but she read in his expression the cool expectation that she would do just that. Pride came to her aid. 'I can't,' she said, 'but I promise I'll be very careful, darling.'

His fingers tightened. He wasn't accustomed to being defied, she realised. Harshly he demanded, 'Is that supposed to comfort me? No *careful* person would have come up here in the first place.'

'Would you drive up here?'

He let her go and walked across to the edge of the little plateau that was the end of the road, looking down a steep cliff. Far below lay a valley, carved out of the volcanic fabric of the island by the heavy tropical downpours of millions of years. A waterfall like a thin thread of silver dashed itself over the cliff, so high that there was no noise drifting up from the valley floor.

Turning back, he said reluctantly, 'Yes, I'd drive up here, and yes, I'm being unreasonable, but—I don't want anything to happen to you, Blair.'

Although his solicitude thrilled some unrenegerate part of her, she was still irritated by his assumption that she was incapable of looking after herself or being sensible where her own welfare was concerned.

'Nothing is going to happen to me,' she said, not trying to hide the tartness in her voice, 'at least, nothing that common sense would prevent, anyway.'

She realised then just how much he had changed, and how imperceptible that change had been. His face stiffened, and once more she saw the man who had watched her that first night, coldly isolated from all around him by his seamless control. The difference between that man and the Hugh she had become used to was so marked that Blair almost gave in.

But she didn't. She was afraid to. She had made a reasonable sort of existence for herself, and if she softened, if she gave him power other than the purely sexual over her, he would take over her life.

'Trust me,' she said, smiling, letting him see that she was not going to be moved.

His brows lifted. 'I have to, don't I?'

But the little spat had spoiled the day. Blair sensed his withdrawal, the clash of barriers locking firmly in place.

That night they made love again with all the fire and need that had built up through the long weeks apart, but although Blair reached the heights of physical ecstasy she was unfulfilled emotionally. He was not rough, but the heart-stopping tenderness of the night before was absent.

The next morning he said, 'I have to go tomorrow.'

Panic flared deep inside Blair. She slid another spoonful of the fragrant apricot flesh of papaya into her mouth. His words, although spoken without expression, had all the weight of finality.

She said calmly, 'What time are you leaving?'

'On the four-thirty plane in the morning.'

So he was going to New Zealand. The papaya tasted like ashes in her mouth but she swallowed it and said, 'It's a totally anti-social hour to leave, isn't it? You'd think they could come up with a better schedule than that.'

'It gets you there in time to do business,' he returned.

Stupid comments, stupid conversation, when she wanted to plead with him to stay, not to be so offended by her need to keep control of her own life...

'So what do you want to do today?' she asked.

He looked at her. 'Hadn't you planned to finish the canvas you're working on?'

'Yes, but——'

His smile was cool, conveying no emotion. 'Then that's what we'll do.'

She hated the day, even though she stuck it out until lunchtime. While she painted on her mountain ledge he read through some technical tome, his silent withdrawal threatening everything she had achieved. It was not just the demand that she stay off the mountain tracks; she could understand that. It was the way he was reacting now because she had refused to do his bidding. He was so strong a character that if she gave in to him she would never be able to call her soul her own.

Intimidated by his aloof, inimical figure behind her, she had to summon all her will-power to concentrate. Perhaps that was why she was a little careless; she stepped back to stare, narrow-eyed, at the sharp line of the hills in front of her, then took another step, and slipped.

It wasn't dangerous. Certainly the slope was steep, but it wasn't a cliff, and she wouldn't have tumbled far. Nevertheless, she called out in shock, and in a blur of movement Hugh had caught her wrist and dragged her back.

Almost immediately he dropped her arm as though it had burned him, and turned away. For long moments they stood silently, Blair absently rubbing her bruised wrist, Hugh breathing heavily until he managed to regain control.

Then, on a note of such savagery that she flinched, he asked, 'Are you all right?'

'Yes,' she said numbly. 'Yes, I'm fine. Thanks.'

She expected to hear him renew his request that she stay off the mountain, but he said nothing, merely went back to where he had been reading in the shade of a somewhat stunted tree.

Biting her lip, Blair looked at her canvas. It was hopeless. She had spoiled whatever she had managed to achieve previously. What glowed sunnily back at her from her canvas was nothing more than a pretty picture.

'We might as well go back,' she said.

Hugh insisted on driving down the mountain, not speaking, his jaw and profile taut with strain. Beside him Blair sat still, wondering why she should want to please him when he had no right to demand anything of her.

Yet when they were inside again she said placatingly, 'I won't go up there again.'

With a remote courtesy that chilled her he replied, 'I had no right to ask you not to. You must do what you want.'

She knew then that her instinct of that morning was correct. He was pulling away from her. Something had happened—surely not just her refusal to let him run her life?—that had made him decide to change the rules.

Pain such as she had never experienced shot through her. Had she been getting too close? She had been wretched before, but always she had been convinced that ahead of her lay happiness if she could only get through the misery of the present. Now she was not so sure; if Hugh insisted on keeping their relationship within the bounds of lover and mistress she might find some sort of contentment. But not even for Hugh could she give up her independence. The prospect of joy and delight that had danced so dazzlingly in front of her for these last few days seemed to have suddenly subsided into ashes.

He kept out of her way while she showered and dressed. The house was very quiet, as though he had left already. Unflinchingly she gazed into the mirror. Pain darkened her eyes with mysterious green shadows, tightened the lush, soft curves of her mouth. Well, she would act with dignity. It was, she thought with a touch of sardonic humour, all she had left now. Now that she was thirty she should probably cultivate it. She was going to need it more and more as the years went by.

They had lunch by the pool, and swam there in the green gloom cast by the creeper instead of the sea, as it was too hot out in the full sun. Then he said that he had work to do, and she said politely that she thought she might rest.

She hoped he'd come to her as she lay on the big bed listening to the drowsy, mournful call of the doves outside, but of course he didn't. The scent of frangipani, soft and sweet, drifted in through the windows. After a troubled hour Blair got up and, sketchpad in hand, went out on to the terrace where he was working.

He looked up, his face expressing nothing but polite interest.

'Don't take any notice of me,' she said, eyeing the papers in his lap. 'I'm just going to do a few sketches.'

He went back to them, forgetting her immediately, his dark brows drawing together as he concentrated. After ten minutes or so she began to sketch him, her fingers moving quickly and competently, trying to use the talent she had to imprison him on paper as he was imprisoned in her mind. She had become accustomed to studying his face in order to understand what he was thinking and feeling, and that careful and intensive scrutiny helped her now.

Eventually she closed the sketchpad and looked away. He was still reading, the arrogant profile slashingly outlined against the sparkling waters of the lagoon. Her hungry heart lurched, almost overwhelming her. She got to her feet and went inside, holding the sketchpad as though it contained details of her guiltiest secrets, and put it away in a secret place with the sketch she had made of him the very first night they had met, and the painting.

They ate dinner late; he was heartbreakingly courteous but distant, as though they had never made love, never touched minds in conversation. Blair followed suit, feeling her heart shatter into tiny shards.

At last, shortly after ten, he said, 'I'll go to bed. I've moved my stuff into the next room so that I don't disturb you when I get up to go.'

Surely he hadn't decided to go, never to come back? Sheer shock made her aggressive.

'Why don't you just admit that you don't want to sleep with me tonight?' she said, daring him.

He lifted his brows, making her feel both crass and crude. 'Very well,' he said coolly. 'I don't want to sleep with you tonight.'

Well, she had asked for it. Or, rather, she had wanted him to tell her that she was wrong, that he wanted her as much as she wanted him. But Hugh was too brutally honest to lie to her.

She drew a short, agonised breath. 'I see,' she said, turning away.

After a moment's silence, he said raggedly, 'It's not going to work, Blair. I'm sorry. I thought it would, but—it won't.'

'But why? What happened?' She had vowed not to ask, not to plead for reasons; dignity, she had promised herself, but dignity was useless. She needed to know why he was rejecting her.

He hesitated, his face rigid. 'I'm just not cut out for a long-distance affair, I suppose. Believe me, Blair, it's nothing to do with you.'

It wasn't the truth, she knew it, but somewhat belatedly pride came to her rescue. 'It doesn't matter,' she said awkwardly. 'Forget I asked. Do you need an alarm clock? I'm afraid I haven't got one, but I could get——'

She was babbling, and he shut her up by saying, 'I've got one. Goodnight, Blair.'

Two hours later she was lying in bed, listening to the waves thunder down on the reef, still wondering, dry-eyed, just why he had so suddenly made up his mind that there was no future for them. Should she have tried to change his mind? No, that way lay only humiliation. He was a man who made his own decisions and stuck to them, and against that stony will-power she was powerless.

Just like a mistress, she thought wearily. A few privileges, no power. How many mistresses had fallen in love with their lovers and hoped for the power that love returned gave them? More than a few.

If only they could have spent this night together...

But she understood a little more of the man she loved now. Once he'd made up his mind that there was no future for them, he would consider making love to be using her. It was a kind of honour, and she supposed she respected him for it, although her body ached with forbidden needs and desires.

She got up and went into the kitchen, poured herself some cool water and drank it, watching the panorama of the skies, the empty, emotionless stars wheeling slowly across the heavy sky, glittering in their formations and colours, heartbreakingly beautiful. A choked sob tore its way up from her chest. She put the glass down and grabbed the edge of the bench, gripping it until her knuckles gleamed white in the darkness, while she fought a brief, savage battle with the desire that throbbed through her.

She couldn't bear it. She wanted him so much, and not just the shatteringly erotic skill of his lovemaking either; she wanted to lie beside him and listen to his breathing, to know she had only to put out her hand to touch him.

Her jaw set. If this was going to be the last night he spent in this house, she was damned well going to make it a night he would never forget.

Moving softly, she went back through the silent house, but instead of going to her own bedroom she stopped outside the door of the room he had chosen to sleep in.

Don't do it, common sense told her. Get the hell out of it! But need and an aching sense of loss drove her to try the handle.

I'll just listen to him breathing, she told herself, knowing that she lied, knowing that she was setting herself up for the biggest rejection in her life, and quite unable to do anything about it. I won't go in, I'll just stand here...

Yet she found herself over by the big double bed, looking down with night-attuned eyes at the man who slept there.

CHAPTER SIX

BLAIR'S heart beat so loudly in her ears that she was sure it would wake Hugh, but he slept on, sprawled across the sheet. As well as the dark mass of his torso and wide shoulders she could see the narrow hips and strong thighs.

Scarcely breathing, she reached out a tentative forefinger to touch the swell of a bicep. He didn't get muscles like that from being a lawyer; he had to do some hard manual work. He could swim like a fish, and there was no mistaking the horseman's configuration, but she didn't know what else he did to keep fit.

She knew so little about him.

But she knew, theoretically at least, how to arouse him. The hours of tuition she had had to endure in the stuffy fortress in El Amir had always been a nightmare to recall. She still shuddered away from memories of the two women pragmatically passing on what she had come to realise were the survival skills for their world, the older insisting the younger translate the explicit directions, their amusement at her embarrassment and her rage, their shrugs when she had demanded her freedom.

Now, as she looked down at the man sleeping in the bed, she wondered whether perhaps she was being given a chance to replace the stifling horror of those days with other memories of a passion that was at least honest.

One of the lessons had been how to rouse a sleeping man so gradually that he had no idea what was happening to him until he was led by the slowest, subtlest of increments to his satisfaction.

Don't, common sense warned. Don't do it! It's perilously close to rape.

But this was going to be the last time. That evening there had been something implacable about Hugh, something that convinced her totally. It was over. He would never come back.

Carefully, she lowered herself to kneel beside the bed.

What followed was a fantasy she had never been conscious of imagining, a breathless, silent seduction that she controlled, she initiated. Her hands moved lightly, stroking him with smooth, sweeping motions, barely touching skin that grew heated and taut from her ministrations. When he had become accustomed to her presence she kissed him, touching the small masculine nipples with her tongue, pulling gently on them, feeling them stiffen in her mouth.

Then she transferred her attention to his navel, exploring the deep indentation, listening to his heart speed up, his breathing increase. Still he made no sound, nor showed any indication that he was awake and conscious of her presence, although he moved restlessly.

Now she used her hair, sweeping it across the flat ribs and stomach, pushing the sheet further down with cautious, trembling fingers so that she could let the warm, silken mass of it lie across his strong, heavily muscled thighs.

He was soon aroused, the thick column of his shaft standing proud from its nest of curls, and so, she realised, was she, almost desperate with a silent, compelling hunger. But before she could satisfy that hunger she had to climb on the bed without waking him.

For a moment she hesitated, but she was in the infertile part of her cycle; the risk was small, almost infinitesimal. Subduing the voice that whispered warnings, she made up her mind.

He was breathing shallowly and fast, almost as though in a fever, and his head was turning from side to side on the pillow, but there was no glimmer beneath his heavy lashes, and although Blair could discern an unfettered desire in his expression she didn't think he was aware of what was happening.

With infinite caution she crept on to the bed, reaching across, easing herself over him. When she was halfway there he swallowed and instantly she lowered her head and stroked her hair across the width of his chest, until she saw his hand clench, and the muscles tighten in his big body.

Gradually, without touching him in any other place, she slid home, enclosing that erect male flesh, taking it deep into her slick, heated sheath. A heavy, shuddering breath lifted his chest, but his lashes remained long and tangled on his cheeks.

The lengthy, subtle preparation had brought Blair's anticipation to a fever-pitch, but for long seconds she was content to just crouch with her knees on either side of his thighs, impaled by him, neither of them moving as they dragged air into lungs suddenly labouring for breath.

She knew what to do. Some of the exercises she had been forced to learn had been specifically to strengthen the internal muscles she was going to use now. Sitting erect and still, she began to tighten and relax those muscles, pulling him further and further inside her.

The sensation was exquisite, slow and sensuous and deliberate, stimulating nerve-ends she hadn't even known existed. Heat began to build, and a yearning for completion, for satisfaction, yet she did nothing else, to all intents motionless, absorbed by the dark countenance of the man she held so tightly within her. Inexorably her internal muscles clenched and unclenched while sensation built and built, became intolerable, agonising, and still she didn't move.

Just before Blair lost control his hands whipped up to her hips and forced her body down, down on to his while his eyelids flew up to reveal slits of dark fire, hot as the blackness on the edge of a lava flow. A miraculous violence exploded within her; she began to shake as rapture roared through her in a shattering contrast to the skilful restraint of her lovemaking.

Almost instantly she was flung up on to another crest of sensation, then another, while he watched, the hands clamped on her hips holding her prisoner, his face a mask of savage, feral satisfaction. She knew when he reached his peak; not even he could conceal such an intense, all-consuming reaction.

Blair's bones wouldn't hold her upright. She collapsed, limp and exhausted, on to him, and lay with the sound of his heart crashing in her ears.

But almost immediately she struggled up. His arms tightened around her. 'No,' he said, his voice guttural. 'You had what you wanted; now you can give me what I want.'

She protested, but he ignored her, and because she felt guilty she didn't protest for long. At least, she told herself it was guilt, for how could she become aroused again after such satiation?

He took his time with her, repeating the leisurely, smooth movements she had used, summoning with devilish skill a tumultuous response. He wouldn't let her touch him, clamping her wrists together on the pillow above her head when she tried, so that her body was open and available like a fair country before a conqueror. His mouth drove her far beyond any other previous experience, until in the end she was pleading brokenly with him to finish, to end the rapturous torment.

At last he did, bringing her to ecstasy over and over again, then with all of his strength thrust into her, taking them both to a climax that annihilated and remade the world. Almost instantly, Blair slipped into sleep, exhausted, slightly sore and strained, locked in his arms.

When she woke she was still in the bed, but Hugh was gone, and the sun was high in the sky. From somewhere in the house she could hear movements and the soft humming that meant Sina was working. Blair stretched, smiling lazily, her body singing in spite of its aches, and then remembrance overwhelmed her and she turned and buried her head in the pillow, shaken and ashamed as she had never been before.

What in the name of heaven had possessed her to go into the room the night before? Lust, she thought bleakly, and a driving, painful need to be close to him one more time. And it was lust that had been satisfied in the hours that followed.

Well, it was over. Blair wanted nothing more than to turn her head into the pillow and wail her despair, but with grim fortitude she forced herself out of the bed. It was no use letting herself wallow in humiliation because she had behaved as badly as any man intent only on his own gratification. She had to go on with her life, such as it was.

It was about as agonising as anything could be. Before, she had managed to find solace in her work. Now, for the first time in her life, Blair came to understand just what loneliness meant. It was not something imposed from the outside; it was a relentless, vicious emptiness that welled up from inside her, tainting her food, leaching away all colour and joy from her life, until she found it difficult to get up in the mornings, and almost impossible to sleep at night. She had thought she missed Hugh before, but this was an agony of soul and mind unlike anything she had ever experienced.

She should be used to it, she thought bleakly. After all, she had coped with the break-up of her marriage, with imprisonment, with Tony's betrayal. But nothing had ever been like this.

Fala'isi had helped her once, given her healing, persuaded her that life could be kind, could be worthwhile. Perhaps it would do the same again.

However, first she had to get over her shame at her behaviour that last time. She had hated the man in El Amir who had thought she was nothing more than a body for him to use, and she had despised the women who colluded with him.

Yet she had imbibed enough of that chauvinist attitude to use her body in exactly the way her captor and the two women he had sent to teach her the finer points of lovemaking thought it should be used. She had rejected their beliefs, but she was no better than they were, for all her liberated standing. She had used Hugh, seduced him into making love when he didn't want to.

And, she thought wearily, she had been punished. So she was just going to have to endure the agony until it faded, as common sense told her it would eventually. In the meantime she worked, striving to use the feelings that tore her apart to some advantage.

She no longer went to the mountains, but began to paint them from below, seeing some affinity with her emotions in the jagged peaks and sharp, time-worn shapes, the sheer cliffs and pillars of ancient lava born in fire unbelievable and now solidified to cold, hard rock. Most of what she produced was useless, but she struggled on, for if she didn't work she would have to think, and that was unendurable.

Each day she swam, striving to exhaust herself so that she would sleep that night, yet most nights she spent hours lying awake in the bed, staring at the stars, trying to keep her mind blank and empty.

The Chapmans were pleased with the painting she did of the light fishers, and paid her a considerable amount of money for it. 'You must come and see it in its new home,' Tamsyn Chapman said over the telephone. 'How about tomorrow? We'll have afternoon tea and talk about New Zealand.'

Blair didn't want to go—the Chapmans were too close to Hugh—but she said, 'Yes, thank you.' Anything to fill her days.

Grant wasn't there, and neither was anyone else, but Tamsyn was easy to talk to, and Blair was roused a little from her apathy.

'I'm missing Louise,' Tamsyn said on a sigh. 'She loves her school, and of course she sees a lot of Hugh and my parents, too, but it's not the same.'

'I gather he lives close to the school.'

'Only a short drive away.' Tamsyn laughed. 'As you may have noticed, she's in love with him, and he's been incredibly kind to her. Well, he would be anyway; he's very good with children. It's such a shame he hasn't any of his own. But I think that he is about to be displaced in her tender little heart.'

Blair smiled as she was meant to, and said lightly, 'Has she discovered boys?'

'Not quite. She's discovered pop stars. Much safer!'

'Ah, I remember hero-worship.'

'So do I. But my heroes were poets, especially Byron.'

Blair laughed. To her surprise it didn't sound creaky. 'Ah, all that dark, brooding wickedness. He has a lot to answer for.'

Yes, it was a pleasant afternoon. She approved wholeheartedly of the position her picture was in and she liked Tamsyn Chapman; in any other circumstances she would have wanted her for a friend.

The next day she hired a little dinghy with an outboard motor from Sina's husband, and took it across the lagoon to one of the tiny motu that dotted the reef, determined to capture the high mountains with the lagoon in the foreground. She set her easel up on the sand beneath a coconut palm and began to work.

It would have been an hour later that she stepped back, gasped as the sand gave way beneath her ankle, and lurched sideways. Her head thumped on to the trunk of the palm, and she was assailed by pain and a hideous splitting feeling as she slid unconscious on to the sand.

She woke to a headache of such monumental proportions that she was sure she was going to be sick, and a sharp, stabbing pain in one of her temples which manifested itself when she moved her head even a fraction of an inch. Her throat was dry, and her ankle hurt unbearably.

The most sensible thing to do was to lie quietly and work out what to do next. Unable to open her eyes against the glitter of the sun on the water and the sand, she tried an experimental wiggle of her foot. Fire shot through it, and she moaned, feeling the sweat run down her temples. As a child she had sprained her ankle once and the peculiar savagery of the pain was firmly back in her memory. For several minutes she breathed slowly, calmly.

Then she forced her lashes up and peered through slitted eyes at the sky. She didn't know how long she had been unconscious, but the sun had moved enough for her to be completely exposed to its rays. If she didn't get into the shade of the scrub she would suffer sunstroke and dehydration at the very least. And even when she was protected by the bushes the sun's rays would reflect off the sea, and she would burn when her sunscreen ran out of efficiency.

What followed was torment. She couldn't get to her feet, so she had to inch herself over the hot, yielding sand. Every movement hurt, but she forced herself to keep going, unable even to grit her teeth because it made her head thump in agonising counterpoint to her breathing. A couple of times she almost fainted, and when at last she had crawled like a wounded animal into the shade her head whirled and for a few seconds she relapsed into unconsciousness.

When she came to she licked her dry lips, but the bag with drinks and food was too far away for her to reach. It wouldn't have mattered, anyway. Even the thought of drinking made her stomach lurch.

Blair lay back on the sandy earth, closing her eyes, and gave herself up to waiting, trying to use as little energy as possible, and refusing to think of what would happen if no one missed her for days.

Slowly the sun dipped westward. She had looked forward to the night, for then she would be cool, but when it came it chilled her, and she shivered and couldn't stop the slow tears that filled her eyes, until she told herself firmly that this wasn't going to help matters. At one stage she used Hugh's name like a mantra, comforting herself with it, but eventually she no longer had the energy, and relapsed into an exhausted doze. Her strength was running out and she could only lie and wait for Sina's husband to realise that something was wrong.

It took him until the sun was high in the sky the next morning. By then Blair was barely conscious, and she remembered, fortunately, almost nothing of what happened after that, although she fretfully resented having her eyelids levered up so that some sadist could shine a light in them over and over again.

Eventually, however, after a nightmare time of thirst and headache, she woke to the realisation that her head no longer throbbed, not even when she moved it, and nobody had shone anything into her eyes for some time. Even her ankle, firmly bandaged, felt almost normal. Her mouth was dry, however, and when she ran her tongue across her lips they were cracked and sore.

'Drink this,' a voice said.

She sucked eagerly on the straw, letting the cool water flow around her mouth and down her parched throat. Then she forced her eyelids open.

Dressed in sparkling white, a nurse smiled down at her. 'Feeling better?'

'Yes,' she croaked.

'Good, because you've got a visitor.'

It was Tamsyn Chapman. She brought flowers in soothing colours of white and cream, and grapes, which must have cost her a fortune as they had to be flown in from Australia or New Zealand, and she only stayed a few minutes.

'Is there anyone we can tell?' she asked after her greeting.

'No,' Blair whispered.

'Your parents?'

'They're in South America. Travelling. They do a lot of travelling. Inca sites this time. Won't be able to reach them.'

Tamsyn frowned. 'All right. We've all been very worried, but you're on the way to recovery now, so you must just concentrate on getting well.' She nodded to the nurse who had clearly given her a sign. 'I won't keep you, but if there's anything you want or need let me know immediately.' Which was kind of her.

Getting well became Blair's sole aim. However, it proved to be easier said than done. By demanding answers she discovered she had suffered a bad case of sunstroke and dehydration and a sprained ankle, as well as mild concussion. Taken separately none of them should have put her in hospital, but together they proved more difficult to throw off. And, although she was touched by the number of visitors she had, inevitably she had plenty of time to think.

It was rather ironic that she should have come so spectacularly to grief on one of the motu that dotted the reef. So much, she thought wryly, for Hugh's fear about her safety in the mountains. The tiny islands were about as safe as any place could be, yet because a seabird's burrow had collapsed she'd ended up in hospital.

Sighing, she looked out through the window at the sheet of emerald and cobalt that was the lagoon, and composed herself to wait patiently for her recovery. It was silly to want Hugh, silly to wake each morning hoping that today he'd come, to be unable to stop herself from sneaking a quick look at each visitor in the hope that this time it would be him. Much more sensible to sink into a lethargy, let the kindly, inexorable regimen of the hospital take over.

Four days later she was more than a little restive, but because she had no one to look after her at home the doctor insisted she stay in the hospital for another day.

At least they let her out of bed, although they wouldn't allow her to get into her clothes. Not that that mattered. All the other ambulant patients were also padding around in sandals and dressing-gowns.

Nobody took much notice when she limped down the long ramp to the grounds, although one of the nurses warned, 'Don't you go too far, now.'

Wondering how far they expected her to get on her crutches, Blair promised not to tire herself out.

It was wonderful to be outside again. Taking deep breaths of the warm air, she made her way to a spot under the wide branches and feathery foliage of a huge raintree, where a seat overlooked the lagoon and the reef. As all hospitals used to be, the one at Fala'isi was built on a hill above the lowlands which the Victorians had considered unhealthy. Although only a short distance from town, it could have been miles away for all that could be seen or heard of the bustling little port.

It was quiet and calm, except for the laughter from a group of nurses who were going off shift. Blair sat very still, listening; she heard the coo of a dove, and another that answered it, the explosive 'put-put-put' of a motor scooter erupting along the road by the coast, and the sound of a car's engine coming up the drive. Threaded through the mundane noises, like a glittering ribbon through simple cotton, was the call of the tikau bird, exquisite cool notes like the chiming of a tiny bell.

Blair stretched her arm out along the back of the seat and turned her face into it, listening with a waiting heart for the call again. It came, and suddenly, astoundingly, she felt the rebirth of hope in her soul.

How strange, she thought wonderingly. Usually she was impressed by visual things, by colour and shape and texture; she loved music, but she wasn't like Hugh, who not only loved it but knew an immense amount about it. He understood the techniques and the theory, and therefore appreciated it far more than she ever could, with her purely emotional reactions.

But the notes of a small bird touched something arid and withered in her heart, freeing her soul from the dark despair that had imprisoned it. Slowly, in spite of her delight, she became aware of the hairs lifting along her spine, along her arms. Almost without volition she lifted her head, and there he was, looking down at her with a hard, still face.

'Hugh?' she breathed, not sure she wasn't dreaming.

His mouth compressed. 'Tamsyn told me on the phone yesterday,' he said harshly, taking a step closer. 'I nearly ripped the bloody telephone out of the wall. Are you really all right?'

His eyes were blue, blue as the lagoon, blue as the depths of heaven, yet the depths were filled with darkness. Blair realised it was fear.

'Yes,' she said quietly. 'I'm fine.' She sat up and touched the seat beside her. 'Come and sit down.'

He shook his head, smiling bitterly. 'I don't dare,' he said. 'I shouldn't have come—I wasn't ever going to come back again, but I had to see that you were all right.'

She held her breath. 'Why?'

'Because I love you,' he said nakedly. 'Because if anything happened to you I'd die.'

Bells should play, she thought dazedly. Fountains should spring into life. Flowers should bloom. Music should roll forth, magnificent and awe-inspiring. Yet all remained still, and the only sound she could hear was the beating of her heart and the clear, evocative call of the tikau bird. Perhaps she should make some sort of study of ancient Polynesian myths; they could well know what they were talking about.

But of course the myth she heard was only that the tikau bird promised the love of one's life. No happiness was mentioned.

'Is that such a bad thing?' she asked at last, when it was obvious he wasn't going to expand on it. Her voice trembled. She felt that she was taking a plunge into darkness, setting off in a dangerous search for unknown, mysterious treasure. 'I love you, too. But you know that.'

His mouth twisted. 'I—I hoped I was wrong,' he said. He looked away, not hesitant, yet clearly unwilling to speak. After a minute he said, 'You can go home if you have someone with you. Do you want me to stay?'

'Do you want to?'

'Yes,' he said starkly. 'Yes, I want to stay.'

Blair's smile was brilliant yet shaky, like that of a young girl when she first tasted love. But once back at the house she didn't know what to do. After that astonishing declaration Hugh had been all efficiency, getting her processed out of the hospital with a speed and charm that surprised her.

There was something different about him. He hadn't altered; certainly the barriers were still there, but there was a change, nevertheless. Blair tried to keep a tight rein on her emotions, but she couldn't stop the way her face softened when she looked at him, and she knew that the nurses and receptionists exchanged smiles behind their backs, knowing and more than a little envious.

As well they might be, she thought dreamily as he closed the door of his hired car behind her. In spite of the leash he put on his emotions, he looked—triumphant, like a warrior who had found the prize for which he had fought.

But she was going to have to be very careful. She wouldn't pressurise him, or try to persuade him into some form of commitment too soon. Whatever had given him such a fear of revealing himself was still there. His avowal of love was a beginning, not an end.

Blair found that slowly walking the short distance to her seat under the raintree had been no real exercise, and to her horror she was almost exhausted when she got inside.

'I told you to wait,' Hugh said, taking the crutches from her. 'I'd have carried you in.'

She leaned against him, grateful for his strength. 'Mmm, you smell nice. I'm far too heavy for anyone to carry, and I'll have to walk around a bit, otherwise I'm never going to get fit again.'

'Your doctor said you were to rest for another two days.' His voice thickened. 'As for carrying you, I've done it before.'

Heat clung to her cheekbones. She made no effort to take him up on the subject, just stood with her forehead against the arrogant jut of his cheekbone. He ran his hands across her back and down her arms.

'You've lost a lot of weight,' he said, almost angrily. 'You're fragile, far too thin.'

She laughed. 'It will go back on again. They did their best to feed me up at the hospital.'

She was not going to tell him that most of the weight loss had occurred before her ordeal on the islet. That came too close to pining away, and she was no Victorian maiden, ready to die for love!

'Mm, good, I like you rounder. My golden girl, sleek and beautiful as a golden panther. I love you so much...'

His voice was deep and intense, more potent than rich wine, and the words he said made her head spin. Weak tears filled her eyes. She gave a sudden, childish sniff, and he laughed softly and kissed her forehead. 'Bed,' he said firmly. 'You shouldn't be standing around.'

'I'm not, I'm leaning on you.'

For answer he did pick her up, and it was only after some hard negotiating that he took her to the terrace and deposited her gently on a chaise-longue. 'Stay there,' he commanded, dropping a swift kiss on her mouth. 'I'll make you a long, cool drink, and we can sit and watch the sun go down.'

'Dinner——'

'Is coming along from the hotel. Tomorrow your housegirl is going to shop in the market for us, and I'm a more than adequate cook, so you don't need to worry about anything but getting better.'

It was worth it, she found herself thinking dreamily a little later. The anguish and the agony were all worth it, just to have Hugh here with her again. She hadn't thought about his astonishing declaration of love—she wasn't able to cope with it yet—but it lay like a diamond in her consciousness, irradiating everything.

After dinner she asked, 'Would you have come back, if Tamsyn hadn't told you I had hurt myself?'

He had been sitting beside her on the wide sofa, looking out across the silver lagoon. Huge cloud banks had filled the sky, and the sun had gone down in a glory of scarlet and crimson and gold, but now the dusk was falling and the colour was all gone except for an after-glow of topaz light on the horizon, transparent and all-pervading. Hugh looked like a statue of some ancient warrior, stern and austere, with only his mouth giving any indication that, like most warriors, he had a softer side to his nature.

'I don't know,' he said slowly, taking her hand in his. Then he smiled, irony and derision blended. 'I'm lying, hiding the truth from myself as well as you. Yes, I'd have come back. I haven't ever been quite so wretched as I was these last weeks. Tamsyn's call only hastened things.'

'Did she call to tell you I was sick?'

He smiled. 'I don't know. Ostensibly she called to talk about Louise—she's at school close to us, and we see quite a lot of her—but I think she knew what she was doing when she dropped her bombshell.'

Something she hadn't recognised eased in Blair's mind. It had been a while since she'd wondered whether he was married, and that casual 'us' must have brought her fears out of the darkroom of her mind where she had banished it, but she simply couldn't see Tamsyn Chapman as the sort of woman who would encourage an illicit affair. The 'us' must refer to him and his housekeeper, the woman who made divine blueberry pancakes.

'I thought you might have taken a thorough distaste to me,' she said carefully, 'because I made love to you that last time.'

'It was the most exciting thing that ever happened to me,' he said, his eyes gleaming.

A sudden pang of need shook her. As though sensing it he carefully tucked her against him, making sure not to hurt her ankle. Blair relaxed into his warm, strong arms. He was not a particularly demonstrative man, so his rare caresses were infinitely precious. But this, she sensed with rising delight, was not so much a caress as a commitment.

'I did take advantage of you,' she said, endeavouring to sound demure, and failing. 'It worried me.'

He laughed softly. 'I woke up the minute you left your room. I didn't move when you came in because I wanted you so powerfully that I could taste my need, I could feel it eating into my gut. What happened blew my mind completely.'

'You louse,' she said, half laughing, half angry with him. 'I've been worrying all this time because it seemed horribly like rape. You'd made it obvious that you didn't want to sleep with me, but I made it impossible for you to say no.'

'I'd have stopped you quickly enough if I hadn't wanted it to happen,' he said. His hand threaded through the silk of her hair. 'It was—I simply haven't the words. One day you must do it again.'

Smiling, Blair touched her mouth to the base of his throat. She had a lot of things to show him, she thought with a suddenly swelling heart. If her two hard task-masters in El Amir were correct, she could give him ecstasy that no other woman in New Zealand, anyway, would be able to do.

In that moment, cradled against him, her nostrils filled with his faint, evocative male perfume, and her heart gently, lightly expanding, the memories of her imprisonment and Gerald's defection were at last robbed of the sting of degradation and fear and betrayal. She was free to be here with Hugh; the techniques that guaranteed him rapture were worth all the fear and anger she had endured during and after her schooling.

Her mother had a saying that, left to themselves, things worked out, a pattern usually evolved. It seemed that she was right.

'I do love you,' Blair murmured.

'And I love you, more than my life, more than anything else, my rarest, most precious jewel.' His beautiful voice lingered over the words, and he tipped her head back, kissing the satiny length of her throat, before finally coming to her eager mouth. 'So beautiful,' he murmured against it. 'And so kind, so sane.'

She wanted him to kiss her properly, to drown in the flood of sensuality, but she had the common sense to realise that she wasn't fit enough to make love. Anyway, this tenderness, so new and rare, was infinitely precious.

'Come on,' he said almost immediately, putting her to one side before he got to his feet. 'I'll carry you into the bathroom, and you can wash, and then you're going to bed.'

'It's too early,' she objected.

He smiled mirthlessly. 'I'm tired. I haven't been sleeping well lately.'

The same irony tinged her answering smile. 'That's funny, because neither have I.'

He was careful with her, even managing to retain command of the situation when he helped her wash, although she tormented him with slow, heated glances and quickly snatched kisses.

Eyes gleaming, he kissed her swiftly, fiercely, then said, 'You're not yet ready for the sort of wild lovemaking we indulge in, so don't tantalise me too much, you wanton.'

She laughed softly and swayed towards him so that her breasts brushed his chest. 'Or what?'

'Or nothing,' he said firmly, wrapping the bathsheet around her with deft movements. 'Do you want me to dry you?'

She leaned her head against him for a moment. 'No, because I've been tantalising myself, too, and I'm really just not ready to make love. My control is pretty precarious at the moment, and if you dry me it may well shatter.'

But he did dry her, then dropped a nightgown over her head. When she had cleaned her teeth he scooped her up and deposited her carefully on to the bed. 'Would you rather I slept in the other room?' he asked, the aloofness she hated stiffening his features.

It eased when she said promptly, 'No, I would not! My ankle is fine, it's not very sore any more, and certainly with the bandage on it isn't going to hurt even if you do kick it. If my memory is any good, kicking is not one of your vices, anyway.'

He smiled. 'No, I don't think it is.'

He showered rapidly, and came back into the room naked.

'Mm,' she said mischievously, running her eyes down his magnificent body, investing the syllable with an unmistakably lascivious intonation. 'I wish I were a sculptor.'

He laughed and switched the light off, pulling her gently across him so that she lay with her head on his shoulder. 'I'm glad you're not.'

'One of these days,' she said, yawning, astounded at the tiredness which rolled over her in great waves, 'I'm going to paint you like that. And I'm never going to sell it.'

'I should hope not.' He kissed her hair. 'I wish I could paint you like that, but your image is so deeply etched in my heart that I don't need the painting. Go to sleep now, my darling.'

She dropped off thinking happily that tomorrow she would discover why he had left her so abruptly both times. Tomorrow was the first day of their life together...

The telephone woke her, ringing insistently while she muttered and groped for it. Unfortunately it was on the other bedside cabinet. 'Hand it over, will you?' she said at last, closing her eyes as Hugh switched on the light.

Without speaking he obeyed. 'Hello?' she said huskily, assailed by the primitive pang of fear that calls in the middle of the night caused.

A startled female voice, middle-aged, answered. 'Could I speak to Mr Bannatyne?' it said. 'Mr Hugh Bannatyne?'

Blair opened her eyes. Hugh was sitting up, his wide, sleek shoulders and chest dark against the white bed-linen. Although a yawn was fading his eyes were alert and watchful.

'It's for you.' She handed over the receiver.

Dark brows drew together in a sudden, forbidding scowl. 'Yes,' he barked. As the woman talked Blair watched his face tighten. A muscle pulled in his jaw. He said in a voice that made Blair shiver, 'How is she?'

The voice at the other end quacked. 'All right,' Hugh said tonelessly, 'I'll be home tomorrow.'

The receiver crashed home and in one movement he was out of the bed. Over his shoulder he ordered, 'Get on to Air New Zealand and tell them I need a seat home on the four-thirty plane this morning. Tell them it's an emergency. Then order a taxi.'

He was in the bathroom before Blair had a chance to ask what was going on. Frowning at the clock, which told her it was three o'clock, she rang the night number of the airline. Five minutes later Hugh had his seat on the jet. A taxi was a little harder to get, but eventually she managed to persuade the night porter at the hotel to organise one of the hospitality cars and a driver.

Pushing her hair back from her eyes, she grabbed her crutch and limped into the bathroom. He had already showered, for his hair was wet. He was shaving; she wanted to ask what the hell was going on, but she caught his eyes in the mirror, and the question died unborn. So cold, so icily distant, he was once more locked away behind the armour of his self-containment.

Blair waited until he put the razor down before asking neutrally, 'What can I do?'

'Nothing.' His voice was hard-edged, level.

Turning, she went back into the bedroom and, with a stomach clenched by a kind of sick panic, repacked his clothes. If only he would tell her what had happened! But then, she thought, folding socks and shirts efficiently, why should he? He might love her, but she was only his mistress.

So much for her tenuous hopes of the night before when she had committed the mistress's cardinal sin and dreamed dreams.

The ache at the back of her throat became painful. She put a trembling hand up to her mouth, biting at her knuckle, but a soft noise in the bathroom made her start guiltily and resume the packing. When he came back into the room she was pulling on a skirt.

'What are you doing?'

She stared at him. He was looking at her with eyes as polished and burnished as the sky in summer; it was impossible to see past that dense, brilliant colour.

'I thought I'd come and see you off,' she said crisply.

'No.'

'I——' She stopped and drew in a shaking breath. He was checking his papers, deftly sorting them, his passport, his cheque-book. There was no emotion in the clean, angular lines and planes of his face, no gentleness, none of the tenderness that had thrilled her so. He looked like a primitive sculpture, everything but one aspect of his character burnished away by the carver's skilful hand, so that his fierce, ruthless will blazed forth.

Blair waited until he had finished then went over and leaned against him, kissing his jaw. 'Darling, tell me,' she murmured, catching fire from his closeness as she always did. 'What is it? What's happened?'

'My wife has had a stroke,' he said, and put her gently to one side, waited with measured courtesy until she had regained her balance, then walked out of the room.

CHAPTER SEVEN

BLAIR made it to the bed, collapsing on to it. The words 'My wife, my wife' drummed hideously in her ears, preventing any sort of thought, anything but a grief so intense that she thought she might be sucked into its black flood and never emerge again.

Nothing had ever hurt like this, nothing, and the fact that it was partly her own fault made it no easier to bear. Motionless as a wounded animal, she lay on the bed that was still scented with his masculinity; when she turned her head she could see the indentation in the pillows where his head had been, the sheets rumpled by his body.

After a time of frozen horror she got to her feet, and hobbled into the bathroom. She felt unclean, so she spent a long time in the shower. It was, she thought dully, a pity she couldn't wash her heart in exactly the same way.

When she came out the sky was alight with the dawn, the sea a still, smooth sheet of dove grey with a pink pathway across it. Blair stood for a long moment, looking at that pathway. It would be so easy to walk into the water and follow that path...

Abruptly realising the direction of her thoughts, she shivered and said aloud, with an attempt at her usual common-sense attitude, 'It leads to the reef, and suicide is a particularly cowardly way out of solving your problems.'

She didn't feel like eating, but she forced down a slice of toast and a cup of coffee. After all, she thought cynically, it isn't the first time it's happened to you. Why not accept that you have lousy luck when it comes to men?

Or perhaps it was some flaw in her character which made her choose the wrong ones. Tony Keeper had been a young girl's love, an infatuation, a teasing, popular playboy. She had been in love with love, intoxicated with her first taste of passion. When she'd discovered his unfaithfulness she had been shattered, but she had refused to marry him even when he had pleaded with her. Either she hadn't loved him enough to trust his protestations of eternal fidelity, or her sense of self-respect had proved stronger than her love.

Gerald had been different. She had been physically attracted to him, but she had been far more attracted by what she had assumed to be his solid dependability, his gentleness. Had she loved Gerald?

No, she admitted now, watching as the sun flung itself exuberantly above the horizon. Transformed into dazzling silver, a frigate bird hung for a second in a crystal globe of light, then swooped out to sea. She followed the rapidly dwindling speck against the cerulean sky until it disappeared.

She had used Gerald, just as he had used her. They had both lied. She had married him because she had thought he was kind and considerate, because the love he'd professed soothed the wound in her heart caused by Tony's duplicity. She had convinced herself that what she felt for Gerald was a more mature emotion, but it had really been a cop-out. And he, while professing his love, had only wanted her. When she could not make love, he had found someone else who could.

Perhaps men just couldn't be faithful. Tony had been driven by a need to prove himself, a true Don Juan, addicted to the hunt; oddly enough, she believed his protestations of love, but, even loving her, he hadn't been able to give up the chase. Gerald had been faithful as long as she slept with him, but his loyalty had gone no further than that. And all the time Hugh had been her lover there had been a wife in the wings.

Poor woman.

Dry-eyed, although the pressure of tears behind her eyes was giving her a headache, Blair picked up her crutch and swung herself into the studio, managed to get her gear on to the lawn in front of the house, set her lips and began to sketch in the scene.

It helped, although it might have been better if she had been able to use the emotions that seethed behind her calm façade. Unfortunately she dared not; they went too deep. So she produced another pretty, vivid acrylic entirely suitable for hanging over a mantelpiece in Auckland or Melbourne or New York, and when she had finished she packed up three that were ready and sent them along to the resort shop with Sina.

Asa was delighted by them, as she always was, sending her compliments with Sam, who drove down and persuaded Blair to go for lunch with him. They ate in the resort dining-room overlooking the lagoon. Sam ignored the beauty outside while he told her the latest episode in his running battle with his wife. All he wanted in reply was soothing noises, so Blair made them, although tension sawed through her. But at last the interminable meal ended, and she was on her feet and ready to go when she looked up and saw Tamsyn Chapman and her husband come into the dining-room.

Tamsyn Chapman said something to her husband. He smiled at her, and she smiled back, and in that moment of communion Blair saw the kind of love she wanted, the kind she now knew she was never going to find.

Pain, sharp and jagged as a spear to her heart, brought her lashes fluttering down to hide the open and complete misery in her eyes.

'What's the matter? Are you all right?' Sam asked, his pleasant face concerned. 'Is your ankle hurting?'

No, my heart. 'Something walked over my grave. Sam, I'd better go; I'm still resting every afternoon, and I'm starting to feel tired.' She even produced a small, entirely artificial yawn.

'OK, I'll get someone to drive you back. You do look a bit pale. You won't mind if I say hello to the Chapmans on the way out, will you? They don't come often to eat here, but they've been invited by a guest, so we've pulled out all the stops.'

She was going to have to meet them. Colour leached from her skin as she went with Sam across the room, forcing a smile. The Chapmans must have known that Hugh was married, yet neither of them had bothered to tell her. They probably thought she knew, so they had a pretty low opinion of her. And that hurt, because she liked them both.

With a head held almost painfully high she smiled, searching each face for some sign of their knowledge, but there was nothing to be gained from Grant Chapman's darkly handsome countenance, and only pleasure and interest from his wife's.

After exchanging greetings, Tamsyn said, 'We're going away for a week or so, but when we come back we must get together, Blair. Don't overdo things, will you? You still look a bit tired.' The note of concern in her voice seemed quite genuine.

Blair smiled, although her lips felt stiff and clumsy. 'No, I won't.'

Grant Chapman looked at her with sharpened interest, but he was too well mannered to stare, and after Sam had exchanged a few words with them they left.

'Nice woman,' Sam said softly. 'He's as hard as nails, but she's a darling. Yet their marriage is sound—well, you only have to look at them to realise that. They'd be good contacts for someone like you, too. They're related to people all around the Pacific, so they'd be a help when it came to making a name for yourself. They've bought one of your paintings, haven't they?'

'Yes, one of the light fishers in the bay.'

'Good.' He opened the door of the car. 'Are you sure you're all right? You look a bit—remote, somehow.'

He saw too much. Blair smiled. Only by distancing herself from her grief could she function, and she was determined not to give in to it. 'I've got a bit of a headache,' she admitted. 'It's probably just the heat and the humidity.'

'Yeah. And that gets worse before it gets better, too. Ah, well, never mind. You get used to it. Am I going to see you at the feast tonight? I could send a car.'

Every week the resort ran a huge Polynesian feast, complete with dancing and the drumming for which the islands were famous. Most of the entertainers were maids and porters at the hotel, or people from the surrounding villages. They were not professionals, but their dancing and singing had a sincerity that was more satisfying than the smoothest of shows.

Fascinated by the contrast between ancient songs and virile dancing, torches and clubs used in mock-warfare with the eminently civilised surroundings, Blair sometimes sketched the event; she had produced several pictures, all of which had been snapped up. In fact, she could probably have painted just that, with each one sold to a member of the audience who turned up on the periphery of her work.

'No, not tonight.' Horror at the thought of it made her speak quickly, clumsily. 'I might go to bed early.'

'Good idea. It doesn't pay to play around with concussion,' Sam said. With his best Bogart leer he finished, 'See ya 'round, kid.'

He was kind. It wasn't his fault that she wanted to scream and smash things, and then weep until she had no tears left.

That afternoon she couldn't settle. Finally she made her way to the terrace, lowered herself on to a lounger and leaned back, staring out to sea with half-closed eyes.

Ever since she'd been on Fala'isi she had enjoyed the island's beauty, and this scene in particular, the green and blue waters of the lagoon shading into indigo by the reef, the line of foam where the huge Pacific rollers shattered themselves to pieces on the unforgiving coral, the several exquisite little motu rising only a few feet above the rest of the reef, their rings of blistering white sand backed by an emerald coating of scrub overshadowed by the feathery heads of the coconut palms.

A small outrigger danced across the waters, potent symbol of the old days when the Polynesians travelled almost all of the way across the huge expanses of the Pacific. Possibly right across and back again, if the kumara, a South American sweet potato which had somehow become a staple of their diet long before any European sailed these waters, was any indication.

But now Blair was enclosed in an icy cocoon. The sun beat down, the little waves ran over white sand and delicate corals where gaudy reef fish swam, on the manicured stretch of beach in front of the hotel people laughed and played in holiday mood, thick foliage grew in tropic profusion on the island's fertile soils, and she couldn't enjoy any of it, not the way the sun glittered across the water, or the powerful contrast of the lagoon with the high, jagged purple peaks in the centre of the island, not any of the aspects of Fala'isi that had so ravished her eyes and emotions previously.

Blair had never known that unhappiness was a physical sensation, that it spread through one's life like a malignant disease. She refused to give in to it, however. Gritting her teeth, she got up and went into the studio. Always, there was work.

It was that thought which kept her going for the next few weeks.

At night, so exhausted that she couldn't stay awake to mourn her dreams, she slept in a different room from the one she had occupied since she'd arrived on the island. She missed the view of the lagoon, but at least it was free of the memories that ate like acid into her serenity.

Her ankle healed, the headaches eased off, and to all intents and purposes she was fully restored to health, apart from an overwhelming lassitude. It took all her energy to fight it, yet when she slept her rest was punctuated by dreams that woke her with their explicitness and anguished intensity.

She arrived home one evening to find a note written in Sina's neat hand. Tamsyn Chapman was trying to contact her. Blair stood looking down at the paper, her eyes fixed absently on a spot of paint on her fingernail. Cadmium yellow, she noted; high on the mountain, where the soil thinned out and the jungle gave way to intense green grass, there lived an orchid with flowers of exactly that colour. It grew nowhere else; remove it from those environs and it died. She had been up there painting it that day.

She liked Tamsyn Chapman, but she found it difficult to forgive her for not saying anything about Hugh's marriage. Gnawing her lip, she threw the note into the rubbish bin. She was hot, the sticky sweat turning silky on her skin. After her shower she would decide what to do about the invitation, if that was what it was.

But even when she was clean and dry and cool she didn't know what her decision should be.

Her hand was steady as she combed out the tangles in her long copper-blonde mane. Perhaps, she thought, repressing memories of how Hugh had loved to bury his face in the flood of it, perhaps she should get it cut. It was a damned nuisance, whipping about her face in the trade winds that blew consistently across the heights. Even tied back into a pony-tail the ends flew about. How would she look with it cut to, say, her jaw?

Who cared?

She put the comb down and left for the kitchen. Tonight she was going to cook herself some fish. She hadn't been eating much of anything except fruit, but that was going to stop. Starving was not going to help anything. She poured a glass of lime juice, touched with a long finger one of the half-dozen or so brilliant, luminous hibiscus flowers that Sina had arranged in a casual, skilful heap on the bench, and wondered despairingly whether she was capable of conveying the satin richness, the gorgeous, saturated colours, as well as their magnificent shape and form. She had tried, several times, but although the results had been competent they hadn't caught the elusive qualities she wanted to convey.

But then, nothing ever did. However complete her vision, the finished work was invariably only a pale echo of it. Smiling ironically, she wondered whether Da Vinci or Picasso had cursed the frailty of his technique, the gap between imagination and the hand that kept those glittering images forever locked in the brain.

Beyond the terrace the lagoon beckoned. The colours of the sea and sky were imbued with some subtle change that wasn't apparent to the brain, although the eye knew instantly that the day was dying. Blair collapsed bonelessly on to the cushions of a wicker chair and tried to work out just what it was that signalled the end of the day—whether it was simply the direction of the shadows, or some mysterious sense, like those possessed by migratory birds.

A small breeze blew up, not cool, but without the humidity of noon. She sipped the lime juice without tasting it. The calm inevitability of the diurnal round should have soothed her, even reassured her, but it didn't. Tension, taut as a wire fence, kept her emotions abrasive and raw.

When she saw him coming along the beach she was convinced that it was merely a hallucination, something her treacherous mind had dreamed up. But as he got closer, walking along the yielding sand with his smooth, predator's stride, a lithe, faintly threatening figure, she realised that Hugh had come back.

Her first thought was joy, pure and unconfined, but it was almost instantly replaced by sheer, brutal fury. Unable to move, transfixed by emotions so strong that she could barely breathe, she watched as he came up the steps and across the grass towards her, his severe face still set in lines of total, complete self-control. He looked, she thought suddenly, older.

'How is your wife?' she asked coolly, marvelling at the voice so like her normal one.

His eyes were hooded, impassive. 'She died.'

Even then Blair had to quell the instinct to comfort him. It made her even more angry. 'I'm sorry,' she said quietly.

He didn't move, but she saw his rejection as plainly as if he had spurned her aloud. She looked away, unable to subdue the volatile mixture of disdain and fury that seethed through her. 'So what are you doing here?'

'I owe you some sort of explanation,' he said.

Blair got to her feet, her usual indolent grace replaced by a jerky speed she hated, because it revealed just how much she was affected. 'You owe me nothing,' she said through her teeth. 'You made no promises, no vows. Just go, will you? I don't want you here.'

He stood looking at her, his eyes so lacking in emotion that she had to stop herself from taking a step backwards. In that moment there was something inhuman about him. 'I'm sorry,' he said unexpectedly. 'I didn't think it would hurt anyone. Just a holiday fling with a woman who was experienced, who knew the score. No one, much less Gina—my wife—would be hurt. Only it didn't work out that way.'

'You bastard!'

Again that shrug, the wide shoulders moving easily beneath the expensive cotton shirt. 'I soon found that I wanted you rather more than was comfortable. In fact, in a very short time I was obsessed with you. And when we finally made love I wanted so much more; I wanted you for my own—exclusive, mine and mine only. We lived in our own private paradise. I should have known the world would intrude, that I'd lose it.'

'Why did you come back the first time?' she demanded furiously. 'If you hadn't come back, I could have——'

'Forgotten about me? Put me down as just another beachcomber's romance?' His smile was cold with irony.

'Yes, that's what I was afraid of. Whatever the danger, I had to come back. And when I did I lost my soul to you, became totally addicted. So I salved my conscience. I told myself I deserved a rest several times a year, that no one would miss me if I stayed a couple of extra days on my way to and from New Zealand—I thought I could have it all.'

'I was your bit on the side, your little bit of crumpet!'

'You are an intelligent, clever, sensual woman, and I loved you. Gina was losing nothing——'

'No!' She turned, her body stiff and erect with antagonism. 'That's how my ex-husband excused his little affair. "You didn't want to make love," he said, so bloody self-righteously, "you didn't want me any more, so it couldn't hurt you if I had an affair with Joanne." I was trying to get myself together, I was trying so hard, and all the time he was——'

Blair stopped, dragging in a breath, clamping down on the pain and the disillusion. 'It doesn't matter. If I'd known you were married——'

'You must have known!' His voice was sharp and disbelieving. 'If not for certain, you must have wondered.'

'Occasionally.' She gave a bitter smile. 'But I told myself that if you were married the Chapmans would know, they'd tell me. I didn't realise your friends don't think infidelity is anything to concern themselves about. Or perhaps you make a habit of this sort of thing?'

'No.' The violence was leashed, pulled under control by his formidable will. He looked at her for a long moment with eyes that were as opaque as enamel. 'You never asked. Any other woman would have asked, but you didn't.'

He was right, of course. Asking, just one simple question, had been the logical thing to do, but she hadn't done it; she had pushed any thoughts of a marriage from her mind.

The fact that he read her so easily only made her angrier, an anger that was exacerbated when he finished savagely, 'What the hell sort of man do you think I am? So undersexed that I'd be content with a week snatched here and there? Why else would I have left you on Fala'isi, if it weren't the fact that I was married?'

Because he didn't love her. That was what she had worried about. Then he had said he did, and she had been so overwhelmed that any concern about his marital status had slipped away. Not only had he used her, but there was the added, wounding complication of his betrayed wife.

'Perhaps I did wonder, deep down,' she said honestly, reluctantly, indignation giving an added bite to her words. 'I suppose I didn't want to face the fact that you might be married.'

Because if she had known there would have been no affair.

'I want you to go,' she said evenly. She looked away, across to the sprinkle of lights that indicated the resort. 'I don't want to see you again, Hugh. You owed me nothing but the truth.'

Her heart was aching, aching, but stronger than that was her fury at being taken for a fool, and a deeper, more intimate pain, because she loved him, and he didn't love her. If he had loved her, he would have told her, let her make the decision.

He didn't plead, of course. After a level look at her proud, adamant face, he said with a return to the old, cold composure, 'Very well, then.' And left her, walking away from her into the thick tropical darkness. This time, she knew, he wouldn't be coming back.

Slowly, almost staggering, Blair made her way into the house.

The telephone rang as she came up to it. Numbly, she looked at it, then reached out a shaking hand to pick it up. Tamsyn Chapman's voice was an unwelcome interruption to the dark misery of her thoughts.

'Shall we make a date for afternoon tea?' she said, and then, clearly taking Blair's silence for acquiescence, 'How about the day after tomorrow?'

'I——' Blair's brain wasn't working, and her tongue felt as though it were made of cotton wool.

'Shall we make it four o'clock? I'll send a car for you.' And she hung up.

Clearly a determined woman, Blair thought hollowly.

By the time the day after tomorrow arrived she was reconciled to going. She made up very carefully, hiding the traces of sleepless nights with a skilful hand, and wore a thin silk dress in a soft peach shade that lent colour to her skin.

The car arrived on time and eventually deposited her outside the long white house where Tamsyn was waiting. They went inside, and ended up in a pretty little room, clearly a boudoir.

'It's lovely, isn't it?' Tamsyn said when she saw Blair looking around. 'Grant's grandmother used it when she was alive. She was French, and it suited her perfectly.'

So it should have. Blair felt slightly faint at the thought of how much the dainty antique furniture was worth.

A maid brought tea in, her long dress swishing slightly on the floor, bare feet silent. Tamsyn poured it, then fixed Blair with a surprisingly stern look. 'What,' she asked, ' have you done to Hugh?'

Blair stared at her. A sudden spurt of anger made her say curtly, 'Nothing.'

'Then why is he looking like death?' Tamsyn sighed. 'Oh, I can see you're still furious with him, but if you blame him for falling in love with you when his wife was alive, don't you think he had some reason? I don't approve of adultery, but who but Hugh would have stayed with her anyway? Or married her, come to that! But he has such a strong sense of responsibility.'

'I don't know anything about his marriage,' Blair said stonily.

Tamsyn's brows shot up her forehead. 'Wouldn't you listen to *anything* he had to say?'

'What could he say?' Blair's voice cracked. 'Believe me, I've heard all the excuses. Just before he left he told me his wife had had a stroke. That was all. It was the first time I'd heard of a wife, and, understandably, I was shattered.'

'Oh, *hell*.' Tamsyn looked directly at her, biting her lip. 'He's made a total hash of everything, hasn't he? Which is surprising, because Hugh doesn't usually do things like that. He knows exactly where he's going and what he's doing. You must have knocked him completely off his feet. Drink up. You look as though you need the caffeine. Perhaps I should get you something stronger to go with it?'

'No, thank you.' Picking up the cup, Blair sipped the tea without tasting anything.

'So you *did* send him away without listening to him.' Tamsyn sounded more than appalled, she sounded angry. 'But why? When he was free of the wretched woman—oh, I shouldn't say that; she was a poor, sad thing and everyone felt profoundly sorry for her, but she had no right to drag Hugh down with her——'

'Look, I said I didn't know anything about Hugh's marriage, and I don't.' Because she liked Tamsyn, and admired her loyalty to Hugh, Blair took a deep breath and moderated her voice. 'Mrs Chapman, it's over, finished.'

'Tamsyn. My name is Tamsyn.' Her hostess looked keenly at her. 'If it's over, why did he come back?'

'He thought he owed me an explanation.' Blair spoke with stony precision.

'Well, so he did. Why wouldn't you listen to him?'

Wearily, Blair told her. 'I can forgive almost anything but lies, and he lied to me all the way through. Oh, he didn't say them out loud, but he implied that he was free.'

'So now you wander around the island looking like a wraith and worrying the life out of your friends and Sina, and Hugh is working himself into the grave in New Zealand.' Tamsyn shook her head. 'Louise spent the weekend at his house, and was so upset by the way he looked she rang up to say he must have been sick and why didn't we invite him up for a holiday!'

'A guilty conscience can take you like that, I believe.'

Tamsyn snorted. 'Why should he feel guilty?'

'Because he slept with me when he had a wife, damn it!' Humilating tears flooded Blair's eyes; embarrassed, she gulped, and blew her nose, fighting for some sort of control.

Tamsyn waited until she put her handkerchief away before saying urgently, 'Look, I can't tell you about Hugh's marriage—that's for him to do—but when he met you it was the best thing that ever happened to him. We were concerned, but we saw the slow, subtle release of the tension he's made part of his character, and honestly, it was like seeing a dry river fill with water. He was almost the old Hugh we used to know. That marriage cost him so much it makes me weep to think of it. He used to be completely different—oh, he was always a formidable, compelling man, with that rather imperious authority, but he used to laugh and he was witty and great fun. Women flocked around him. Well, they still do, of course, but he was immensely, blazingly attractive, almost irresistible. Over these past six years we've watched him retire further and further into his shell, and it's been hell for all his friends.'

'For his wife, no doubt, as well.'

Tamsyn flung up her hands. 'All right, I don't blame you for being bitter; he should have told you, but I think he was afraid.'

'Hugh? *Afraid*?'

'He's just a man,' Tamsyn said forthrightly. 'In spite of that rigorous control he suffers and feels and bleeds like the rest of us. Loyalty is important to him, and he suffered, knowing that Gina would hate the fact that he had found you.'

'Any wife would.'

'Yes, but Gina had no right to!'

Fighting an incipient headache, Blair pressed the heels of her hands to her temples. 'That's a strange thing to say,' she muttered. 'Most women would feel they had every right to object to their husband having an affair. I know I did, and I suppose for my ex-husband there were extenuating circumstances. He certainly thought there were!'

Tamsyn frowned. 'I didn't know about your ex-husband, but Hugh is different. Oh, what a shambles!' Her voice turned coaxing. 'Blair, couldn't you listen to him, at least? You're dealing with a man so hung up on his honour and his integrity that he despises himself for snatching at happiness.'

'I despise him too,' Blair said fiercely. 'He stole it, he didn't snatch it.'

'And I suppose you told him so?'

Blair shrugged. 'Not in so many words, but I'm sure he got the message.'

The older woman sighed. 'So he's convinced that you're not ever going to forgive him. Can't you meet him halfway?'

'I'm not a halfway person, I'm afraid,' Blair admitted, setting her cup and saucer down. A dreary grey tiredness welled through her.

'I'm sure it's all a misunderstanding. You must talk to him. It's *vital* that you listen to what he has to say.'

Blair ran a shaky hand through her hair, holding it up for a second from her hot nape. 'It wouldn't do any good,' she said wearily. 'It's over.'

'Well, I tried,' Tamsyn sighed. 'I hope you don't ever regret this.'

Blair's shoulders lifted fractionally. 'So do I.'

But when she was back home once more she sat for several minutes, staring moodily at nothing in particular. Had she been too quick off the mark when Hugh came to see her? Should she have let him try to explain? She just didn't know. And she was afraid to listen to him, in case she surrendered to a man she could no longer trust.

On her way up from the beach the next day, she was examining a rare pink shell she'd picked up from the sand when she heard someone call out from the other side of the house.

'Blair! I say, Blair Doyle! Anybody home?'

The woman who waited at the front door was tall and thin and angular, dressed in a smoky pareu of lilac and mauve and grey. Huge silver earrings and a handful of rings, most of them chosen, Blair decided after a quick look, for their eye appeal rather than their intrinsic worth, added a touch of exoticism to her appearance.

Blair felt scruffy and salty and sandy, but she smiled and met the eyes so frankly appraising her. 'I'm Blair Doyle.'

'Well, if you can really paint, we've got it made,' the newcomer said, astonishingly. 'Mind you, looks like that will sell the things, even if you can't paint. But if that's so I won't act as your agent.'

Blair's brows shot up. The other woman grinned and held out her hand. 'I'm Rilla Baker, and I own a gallery in Auckland. I'm staying at the Coral Sands, and when I showed some interest in your work—I said it was a pity you weren't doing something that used all your intelligence and talent—the woman in charge of the shop there insisted that you were, and sent me on down. Was she sending me on a wild-goose chase?'

Blair shook hands with her, feeling rather as though she'd been thrown in front of a steamroller. However, for the first time since the telephone call in the middle of the night, she felt stimulated.

'You'd better come and have a look,' she said drily.

'I was hoping you'd say that.'

Rilla Baker looked through the canvases quickly, but her speed didn't fool Blair. Clearly she knew exactly what she was doing; she made several small murmurs of appreciation, frowned over a couple of others, looked neutral with very few, and in each case her opinion coincided with Blair's.

'OK,' she said when she had finished. 'Yes, we can do something with those.'

Before she could go any further, Blair said, 'You do realise that I'm known in Auckland as a decorator?'

'Decorator? As in houses? Sofas shaped like mouths, all that jazz?'

'Not quite. I was a partner in Decorators Inc until last year. We didn't go in for mouth-shaped sofas.'

'Ah. Tegan Sinclair's firm? I've seen quite a bit of your work, then. I like the style. Restrained yet interesting, and always keeping in mind that a house is a place to live. You don't try to copy what's just come out in the overseas mags. Hmm, what's being a decorator got to do with the fact that you're not contracted to a gallery?'

Blair shrugged. 'It doesn't give me much credibility in the art world.'

The gallery owner's shrewd brown gaze went to the canvas she had last looked at—a tempestuous thing of waves and winds and waters. She made a sudden, decisive gesture.

'It's only going to concern the occasional purist. Ignore it. I want you to join my group of younger artists, Blair Doyle. I think you've got what I'm looking for. Do you want to go the hard way with lawyers, or are you happy with a handshake?'

'One thing earning my living as a decorator taught me was caution. I like things to be signed and sealed. Tell me what you're offering.'

'Caution, and a good business head. I like that. A lot of artists think either is beneath them, and that makes my life hellishing difficult sometimes. OK, we do a showing first, then I'll take everything you can produce. Not the sweetly pretty things—thank God you used a different name for those; they won't drag the value of your real stuff down.'

Her terms were conventional. Blair had every intention of checking her out, but she liked the woman and was disposed to trust her. 'That sounds fine,' she said, adding, 'However, I'd like a written agreement.'

'No problem. I happen to have one in my bag.' She began to fossick in the depths of her bag.

Blair's brows shot up. 'Did you expect to find a painter for your gallery up here?'

'I never waste an opportunity,' Rilla Baker said, smiling a touch secretively.

Blair nodded. 'I'll let you know definitely tomorrow.'

'Fair enough.' The older woman looked around. 'This is a nice place. Is it yours?'

'No.' Blair explained what she was doing there and the other woman sighed.

'Amazing how some people fall into luck. How long are you here for?'

'Until the end of the year.'

'That's fine. You can get this out of your system—we'll call it your tropical period—and then you can start on an Auckland period. Aucklanders like buying pictures of Auckland. I'll be down at eleven tomorrow morning.'

Blair looked at the business card in her hand, watched the thin figure of the gallery owner stride down the path, and wondered whether she had been dreaming. An Auckland period indeed! If Rilla Baker thought she could tell her what to paint, she had another think coming.

Smiling ironically, she made her way to the telephone.

Half an hour later she put the receiver down. Tegan had not only heard of Rilla Baker, she had been enthusiastic, but just to make sure that Blair wasn't taken advantage of she had put Kieran on the phone. He'd gone through the contract with her, clause by clause, before telling her to sign nothing until he'd had a chance to investigate the woman.

'Fax a copy down to me and I'll have a solicitor look through it,' he commanded.

Another powerful man, she thought drily as she hung up. Kieran's only weakness seemed to be his wife, whereas Hugh clearly hadn't worried a bit about his.

What sort of marriage had it been? Judging by Tamsyn Chapman's references it hadn't been conventional. A poor, sad woman, she had called his wife. And she had been rather alarmingly certain that it didn't really matter if Hugh committed adultery. Which surprised Blair. From the little she knew of the lovely and gracious Mrs Chapman she would have thought she had high standards when it came to personal integrity.

But whatever anybody said, whatever the circumstances, they couldn't alter the fact that Hugh had married Gina, and that he owed her his loyalty. She might have been a poor, sad creature, and their marriage far from normal, but she had been his wife.

Blair bit her lip against the pain and tried to think of something else.

Kieran rang the next day, not only telling her that the contract seemed a reasonable document, but that Rilla Baker's name was crystal-clear, both for integrity and for having a nose for good new artists, most of whom were pleased with the way she was developing their careers.

'So you think I should sign it?'

'That's entirely up to you,' he said, 'but there's certainly no reason that I can think of for you to feel dubious about it. The woman is honest, and she has a good reputation both with artists and the art world—which is, I gather, unusual.'

'OK, then, I'll sign it. Thanks for all your work.'

'*De nada*.' He sounded amused. 'I have to do my best for my heir's godmother.'

'You're convinced it's going to be a boy?'

'What a sexist remark, Blair. Why shouldn't a woman own a merchant bank?'

They laughed together, and after saying goodbye she hung up, trying to ignore the odd sense of loss she always felt when she thought of Tegan and Kieran's marriage. Although it probably wasn't loss; more like envy, she thought sourly.

Rilla Baker was pleased with her decision to sign, and treated her to lunch with champagne, after which they got down to business.

'I want to mount an exhibition in six months' time,' she told Blair. 'Small but exclusive, and only your very best work, mind you. I won't be fobbed off with the second-rate. I'll start the publicity as soon as I get back. I think you've got the potential to turn into a very fine artist.'

A year ago those words would have made Blair ecstatic. Three months ago they would have filled her with delight. That they didn't now was yet one more thing to blame Hugh Bannatyne for.

She said, 'I hope I do.' Because it looked as though her art was all she was going to have to keep her company for the rest of her life. And her friends, of course; she thrust self-pity back down into the depths where it belonged.

'I'm not in the habit of backing losers,' Rilla said firmly. 'Not even . . .' Her voice trailed away.

'Not even——?'

'Oh?' The older woman sat up, looking across the other side of the room. 'Sorry, I thought I saw someone I knew, but I was mistaken. No, I have a certain reputation to keep up. People are beginning to realise that at my gallery they can find work they really like, work that satisfies the mind and the emotions as well as the eye; from someone who isn't too expensive, someone who has staying power and who's likely to make some sort of name for themselves in the art scene in New Zealand. I guard that reputation.'

It was an oddly impassioned little speech, the cheerful, rather ostentatious mask of bohemianism dropped for a moment to reveal the earnest woman behind.

'I'm sure you do,' Blair said swiftly.

'Right, well, that's settled. I'll take all your stuff. It'll need to be framed properly, of course. What sort of frames do you want?'

They discussed frames for a while, and then it was time for Blair to go. 'Enjoy the rest of your holiday,' she said when she had thanked Rilla for the meal.

'I'm going back on the four-thirty plane tomorrow morning,' Rilla told her with an expressive grimace. 'You just keep on painting, dear girl. Concentrate on the Past Lives series. That self-portrait of you in the hole is truly something, and the mountain batch are good, too. I want more of that sort of thing. Oh, and I like the flowers as well. Of course they're the more easily accessible. They'll go like hot cakes. Keep it up, and get some more sleep. Bags under the eyes don't suit you.'

Blair laughed.

'That's the first time you've actually done that,' Rilla said, her dark eyes twinkling. 'It suits you.'

'Thank you. Safe journey back.'

'You too.'

But there was not, Blair thought wearily as she trudged along the beach, any likelihood of a safe journey back for her. It had been over two months since Hugh had flung his bombshell at her and walked out of her life, and she still longed for him. Instead of easing the ache had grown stronger, so that she dreamed of him at night, still woke in the morning with her arms outstretched.

Fala'isi had seemed like paradise to her, but she had lost it now, and when she looked at the future she saw only the pain that must have eaten into the hearts of Adam and Eve when they too had been thrown out of their Eden.

CHAPTER EIGHT

'ALL right,' Rilla said firmly, 'that's it. It's been a howling success but now it's time to go home.' She beamed around at the few people left in her gallery. 'Almost three-quarters of them sold, and old Firkin muttering about a new Rita Angus! Darlings, I give you one last toast——Blair Doyle!'

They drank, and Blair, a smile warming the cool green of her eyes, thanked them, but said obstinately, 'I am nothing like Rita Angus, and my work is not like hers!'

'Of course you're not, and it's not, but Firkin's on the right track—you've got that instantly recognisable touch. Blair, why don't you take Mrs Sinclair home now? And yourself, too. You look exhausted, and your friend is far too close to profit for my comfort.' Her smiling gaze encompassed Tegan's tall, pregnant figure with just the right hint of wariness.

Everyone laughed, but they did break up at this, and soon Blair and Tegan were back in the beautiful, extremely comfortable old house where the Sinclairs lived. Kieran, who had been called away to an urgent meeting with someone from the government, arrived home as they sat drinking herb tea and hashing over the evening. He listened with every appearance of interest to Tegan's excited commentary, promised to go in the next day to see the showing, and somehow, without saying a word, managed to get his wife to bed within ten minutes of his arrival home.

The man had style, Blair thought as she closed the door into her bedroom. Normally she would have stayed with her parents, but they were travelling once more, this time on the Silk Road somewhere between Pakistan and China, so the house was shut up.

In a way she was glad. At least she didn't have her mother worriedly asking her what the matter was. Beyond giving her a sharp look when she met her off the plane, Tegan hadn't revealed any alarm at her friend's too-slender contours, or her stringently disciplined features.

Yawning, Blair got out of her clothes, creamed the cosmetics from her face, and climbed into an oversized T-shirt. She had just settled into her bed when there was a tap at the door, followed by Tegan, swathed in a silk nightdress that somehow managed to make her look both maternal and alluring. Blair decided to paint her like that and give the canvas to Kieran as a Christmas present.

'Damn,' Tegan said, her smile evident in her voice, 'it just isn't fair! You look like a million dollars, while I'm the shape and size of a small submersible. I'm so glad it went off so well. I feel terribly impressed and awe-struck to have such a famous artist as a friend.' She grinned mockingly.

'Rubbish. You've got *me* as a friend, that's all. One rather successful showing doth not fame make.' Because she was touched, Blair's voice was more acerbic than normal.

Tegan sat down on the end of the bed. 'I'm glad you gave us first pick. I just love those hibiscus flowers—it beats me how a picture of flowers can somehow convey the mystery and terror of the South Sea Islands as well as the overwhelming glamour and beauty, but you've managed to do just that. I always knew you were clever, but I didn't know just how much. Are you happy, Blair?'

They'd known each other far too long for Blair to get away with a lie. 'More or less,' she said calmly. 'Contented is a better word, I suppose. I still miss Hugh just as much as I did six months ago when he walked out. I have the awful suspicion that I'm going to miss him for the rest of my life. It must be like this when someone you love dies.'

Tegan sighed, smoothing her hand absently over her distended stomach. 'It's part of the price you pay when you love someone. If anything happened to Kieran... Well, it's not likely to. Blair, are you just going to let the man go? That doesn't sound like you; you've always been a fighter.'

Blair shrugged. 'If I thought there was any prospect of happiness for us I'd give it a go, but he lied to me. I was just his mistress, and I've had enough of that sort of behaviour.'

'Did you ever tell him about Gerald? And that nasty man in the Middle East?'

'Gerald, yes, but not the other. And he wasn't really nasty. Just—different. What would be the use?'

Tegan frowned, watching her friend's face with far too sapient an eye. 'At least he'd understand why you reacted so violently to his lies.'

'I think I had every right,' Blair said wearily. 'Whatever excuse he had, he was married. He owed his wife his loyalty. Anyway, it's over.'

'I hate to see you so unhappy.' Tegan glowered. 'I'd like to give that wretched man a piece of my mind. You've had a rotten three years, then you had to top the whole wretched business off by falling in love with a philanderer! It's the purest bad luck!'

Warmed by her partisanship, Blair smiled and touched her hand. Tegan's returned the pressure. They sat a moment or two, until Blair said crisply, 'It's not the end of the world. Other people have fallen in love with the wrong people, and I seem to make a habit of it. I'll get over it.'

'Of course you will.' But Tegan didn't look convinced. She said, 'Only it cut deeper this time, didn't it?'

'Yes,' Blair said simply. 'I'd never felt anything like it before. It was like a transformation. But you know about that.'

Tegan smiled and got to her feet. 'Yes,' she said softly, 'I know about that. I hope it all comes right for you, too. You deserve to be happy.'

'Does anyone, ever? Happiness is just a matter of chance. Go to bed; it's too late to be discussing philosophy, and if I know Kieran he's going to come looking for you in a few minutes.'

'He's a bit over-protective,' Tegan admitted, but her glowing, tender smile made it clear she didn't mind.

When she had left Blair switched off the light and lay back. She had never hoped for a showing as successful as this one had turned out to be. All her expectations were surpassed. She should be pleased; damn it, she *was* pleased, yet this ever-present agony of loneliness smudged the bright pattern of her success.

Hugh as a lover had been all that any woman could hope for, yet that was not why she missed him. He had got so far beneath her guard that his presence had diminished the existential solitude of every human being. With him she had felt a little less alone. Just knowing that he existed in the world had been enough to comfort her.

She had given him her love, only to discover that it was tainted, that his loyalty and his life were devoted to his wife—— She bit her lip, hating the tears that came so often in the darkness, aware that she had to get over him. The last six months had been busy and productive, yet she was still aching with a cold emptiness, the small triumphs and griefs of her life overshadowed by the greater loss of the only man she had ever loved.

The man who had said he loved her. That was what hurt. He'd fooled her into believing him, which made her such a blind, gullible idiot.

However, she was not going to let this ruin her life. She was capable of dealing with it; she would make herself a successful, happy existence without Hugh.

But oh, God, when would the pain go away?

At breakfast the next morning Tegan thrust the newspaper at her, saying, 'The review is excellent, although he does compare you to Rita Angus. Not in style, however, only in that you both have a totally individual vision.'

Blair absorbed the review. 'Well, I'm astounded,' she murmured. 'And not a word about being a decorator.'

'Why should there be?' Kieran asked drily. 'Apart from showing that you have an artistic eye, is it relevant?'

'Come on, Kieran, you know as well as I do that relevance has precious little to do with most reviews!'

He laughed and got to his feet, bending over to kiss his wife. 'Don't overdo it,' he commanded. 'I'll see you both tonight.'

Tegan went out to see him off. When she reappeared Blair asked, 'What are you doing today?'

'Oh, I've a busy morning ahead. Visit to the doctor, so he can take my blood-pressure and listen to the baby's heartbeat and tell me I'm disgustingly healthy and it won't be long now, then a conference with Andrea at the office, then a small amount of shopping. When are you due at the gallery?'

'At ten.' Blair hid a yawn. 'Though I think I'll go in half an hour earlier. I want to wander through and really look at all the ones I've sold. I don't suppose I'll see many of them again.'

'I'll see you this afternoon some time, then?'

'Yes. Rilla's taking me out to lunch; she wants to discuss what she insists on calling the plan of battle. It won't take more than a couple of hours, so I should be back halfway through the afternoon.'

After Fala'isi Auckland was too big, and the streets seemed more crowded than they had before she left for her lovely, lost paradise. Blair drove the small car she had hired for a week through the central business district and into the basement car park of the high-rise that held the gallery.

She loved Fala'isi, but she realised now that she wouldn't be sorry when it was time to leave. Somehow the island's beauty, its welcoming ambience, had become tarnished by Hugh's betrayal.

The double doors to the gallery were still locked. Of course, it didn't open until ten. Irritated, Blair turned back to the lift, waiting unsummoned by anyone else, then changed her mind. Rilla's office was just down the corridor; she'd go in through there.

Unless it was locked, too. No, it was slightly ajar, so Rilla had to be there. Blair lifted her hand to knock, then froze. A voice she recognised said something indistinguishable, answered by Rilla's clearer, sharper tones.

'Look, Hugh,' she was saying, 'I know my job. I trusted you when you said she was good, now you tru——' She stopped, her mouth dropping open in shock. Blair pushed the door open the rest of the way and stood like a stone statue, her green eyes freezing to chips of glass in a white face as she realised who was standing there with Rilla, and what his presence meant.

It was all lies.

Hugh had sent Rilla to Fala'isi with instructions to sign Blair up as one of her stable. No doubt, Blair thought, bitterness expanding through her, he wanted to get her safely settled so that he didn't have to feel guilty about her any more.

Hugh's head jerked around. Shock and dismay shattered the controlled mask of his features. Choking back the tide of nausea that rose high in her throat, Blair whirled about and raced for the still stationary lift, intent only on getting away before she had to say something, before they tried to justify what they had done to her. She couldn't cope with that. The thought of being patronised raked across her pride with tines of poisoned steel.

'Blair! Stop that!'

Hugh's voice, deep and shaken, and definitely uttering a command. She ran faster, but although her heart was beating too heavily in her ears for her to hear him she sensed his rapidly closing presence.

Miraculously, the lift hadn't moved from its position. Hurtling in, she jabbed the button to close the doors, immediately pressing the other one that took her to the basement. The car park was empty. Frantically, she ran across to the car and was almost there when she saw Hugh race like an avenging demon down the stairs. Gasping, absurdly afraid, she wrenched the door open and fell in, locking the car, turning on the engine. Relief raced through her as it fired immediately and, clashing the gears, she drove dangerously off. When she got to the entrance there was no sign of him, or any car. A shuddering breath hurt her lungs; she relaxed a fraction, setting off for Remuera.

Of course he wouldn't follow her. What would be the use?

Deliberately emptying her mind of everything but the need to concentrate on the road, she negotiated the inner-city tangle. But just in case he had come after her she drove into the Domain and stayed there, huddled for an hour on a seat beneath a huge Moreton Bay fig tree, watching with unseeing eyes the harbour glittering with deceptive promise beyond the business section of Auckland. She tried to gain control of the riot of emotions that tormented her, but she could only dwell on the acid fact of betrayal.

Fool, fool, *fool*! She had done it again, allowed her wishful thinking to persuade her into folly. At least she would have time to gain control of herself, time to work out what she had to do, before Tegan came home.

But as she was inserting the key in the lock at the Sinclairs' house she heard the sound of a car coming up the drive. A horrified glance over her shoulder revealed a big BMW with Hugh behind the wheel.

Panic made her witless; she ran inside, flinging the door closed, but it didn't snick, and the footsteps behind her didn't hesitate as he came into the hall. Without thinking, compelled by a totally mindless fear, she raced up the stairs, intent on getting to her room. She could lock that door.

He was close, though. His breathing resounded harshly in the quiet house. Panting, a red mist in front of her eyes, she managed to reach the door before him, even slam it shut in his face and turn the key in the lock.

'Open this bloody door!' He spoke in a voice she didn't recognise, a voice filled with fury and savage, implacable command.

Her fingers trembled; in spite of that she yanked the key out and stood staring at the door with eyes that were far too big for her face.

'If you don't open it, Blair, I'll break it down.'

Without volition she took two steps backward, but after a second her panic died. No, Hugh wouldn't do that. He was always so totally in control, there was no way he'd smash down someone else's door.

'For the last time, Blair, open the door.' His voice was soft and deadly.

He was trying to intimidate her, to bluff her into opening it. Mutely clasping her hands to steady them, she waited tensely for him to go away.

A splintering crash made her gasp. 'Stop it!' she whispered, eyes dilating endlessly.

'Open the door!'

But Blair was beyond responding. She could only stare with stunned, disbelieving eyes while he kicked the door in and came through, breathing deeply as he pushed a lock of hair back from his forehead.

'Get out,' she croaked in a trembling voice.

He kept on coming, filling the room with his presence, watching her with that intent, predator's gaze. Made mad by a mixture of shock and fear, her heart thumping sickeningly in her throat, she hit out at him. He smiled, the cold, patient smile of a huntsman, and grabbed her arm, pulling her hand away from his face with insulting ease.

'That isn't going to get you anywhere,' he said.

From somewhere, Blair summoned her usual resolve, snarling between her teeth, 'Get the hell out of here, or I'll—I'll——'

'You'll what?' he demanded insolently. 'Throw me out? Try it, Blair.'

'Are you mad?'

'Quite possibly.' He watched her closely as his hand slid up her arm and the other came around to hold her still.

'No,' she cried, seeing desire flicker in his eyes.

She tried to take him by surprise, but he was waiting for her, and the movements she had learnt in self-defence lessons were remorselessly countered. He was big and strong, and he was ruthless, not caring that he hurt her. Yet when she lay panting in his arms he bent his head and kissed the inchoate bruises, his mouth lingering on her smooth skin.

'Don't fight me,' he whispered. 'I don't want to hurt you.'

'You're always hurting me.' She had to talk him out of it before he did this and crushed her memories of love into small, tarnished shards. 'I don't want you, Hugh.'

'No?' He was smiling.

When she opened her mouth to swear at him he kissed it, seducingly sweet, and then fiercely, with a passion he made no attempt to hide.

Half sobbing, Blair kissed him back, the traitor within overcoming all the resentment and pain, the practical common sense that should have thrown him out. It was heaven after all these months, and if she was a fool for surrendering, then she would worry about that afterwards.

It was the last coherent thought she had for long minutes. He had been a virile and sensitive lover, but always before she had been aware of the barriers, of the fact that he had to control even that part of their life together.

She sensed the difference almost immediately, recognised the wild hunger he made no attempt to curb in the way his hands trembled as they sought the hidden places of her body, the heated skin and hard flexion of his muscles when she touched him. He was beyond restraint, locked in a need so powerful and violent that he was completely unable to leash his responses.

He tore her clothes from her, and then his own, and she didn't try to stop him—she needed it just as much as he did, this furious yielding to desire. Dimly she realised that her hands on his body were inciting him, her voice was whispering broken commands, love words, dark, potent words that made him groan.

When at last he moved over her she cried out, and the first violent thrust of his body should have hurt, but she was ready, she arched to meet it, her eyes frenzied, her mouth soft and swollen and red from his kisses, her body aching with a wholly merciless need. It was dangerous, it was heaven, it was all she had ever wanted from him, a total merging of bodies and spirit that took her into another realm entirely.

Always before he had made sure that she reached her satisfaction before he took his own, although usually they came so close together it was almost simultaneous. But this time he drove deep into her as though hounded by demons, and the powerful force of his body so excited her that she shuddered and came, and then just as she began to float down his anguished groan sent her spinning up again, captured by waves of rapturous sensation that flooded through her body.

The instant he came, as she felt the rigors shuddering through him, Blair realised that something had altered so irrevocably there could be no going back.

Gasping, she dragged breath into her lungs, waiting for her heart to slow down, for the sweat to dry on her body. It seemed like the most bitter betrayal that his lax weight on her should feel so wonderful, so right.

He had, she thought bitterly, almost raped her.

No, he hadn't. She had behaved like a wildcat, and he'd only taken what she'd offered. Somehow this made things much worse.

Harshly she demanded, 'Why don't you buy a woman, for God's sake? That's all you want, someone warm and willing to take to bed. There are plenty around who'll give that to you. Why steal the reluctant response of my body from me?'

'Reluctant?' He rolled over on to his back beside her, but not before she had seen the sudden pain in his face.

Angrily glad that she had managed to crack that iron-bound composure, even if it was only for a second, she said, 'I didn't want this.'

'You're trying to convince yourself.' His voice was firm and definite. 'No other man could do that for you, just as there's no other woman who makes me feel like that. I want you, not just the physical release. I want to hear you laugh, to wake in the morning with you, to talk to you and warm myself in your kindness and your intelligence and the intense fire you try so hard to hide behind that mask of indolence and laughter, so that only those who buy your paintings know it's there.'

'So you want the artist?' He seemed to mean what he said, but she was still afraid. 'All artists don't lead bohemian lives, you know. I won't be your mistress again.'

'I know,' he said quietly, still staring up at the ceiling, his arrogant profile outlined against the wallpaper, the straight forehead, the strong nose, the clean moulding of his mouth and the autocratic line of his jaw. Only the soft curve of lashes gave any hint of gentleness to his face. 'If I thought you responded like that to every man who looked at you and wanted you, believe me, you wouldn't see me for dust.'

'You don't know that I don't.'

He laughed. 'Blair,' he said, his beautiful voice raw with the lingering remnants of passion, 'if you were promiscuous, you wouldn't be trying so damned hard to persuade me that you are! I know you don't sleep around. I knew it before we made love that first time. I should have left you alone, but I wanted you so much that the principles I'd lived my life by until then suddenly meant nothing to me any more. I was so afraid of losing you. And you wanted me too.'

'No,' she whispered.

'You're lying again. Your pulse is throbbing like a trip-hammer in your wrist, in your throat.'

'Why did you go?' she blurted out. 'After we made love that first time—and then after I slipped, up on the mountain. Why?'

'The first time I knew I was in trouble. You were all that I had ever wanted—and I knew I couldn't have you. Ever. I couldn't divorce Gina.'

Gina? Blair's breath clogged in her throat. Gina, whose name he had said so unemotionally, his *wife*.

'So I ran away from temptation. But I couldn't stay away. The second time?' He smiled sardonically. 'That was when I realised I loved you. I saw you slide over the edge, and I thought, My God, there goes my life! I was terrified, because I've never given any woman that sort of power over me. I left you because I was a coward. And because you deserved so much more than anything I could give you. I had no right to keep you tied to me for years, perhaps, when I couldn't offer you anything more than a long-distance affair.'

'Surely that decision was mine to make,' she said coldly.

'I didn't want to see you grow bitter, as I was growing bitter, to want more than I could ever give. You deserved a husband, and children, you deserved happiness, and peace—all of the things I couldn't give you. What would your decision have been?'

She swallowed. Her mouth dried suddenly so that the words were harsh and constricted. 'I don't know, do I? You took the right to make it away from me.'

'I behaved like a fool. A fool and a coward. I've missed you,' he said inexorably, his mouth twisting. 'Being away from you is like dying of thirst, like longing for green grass in the desert, like the memory of summer to a man freezing in a glacier. I can't sleep without dreaming of you, and I can't get any work done because you stand between me and everything else. I think I'm addicted to you.'

Addicted. The word echoed so painfully in her heart that for a long second she couldn't speak. He was turning his head when she said remotely, 'Addictions are bad for you.'

'Are you telling me you don't feel the same way?' His voice was bland.

'I can't say that I don't want you,' she admitted unevenly. 'I just don't think it would be a good idea.'

'Why? Is there another man?'

She should say yes, but she couldn't lie to him. 'No.'

'I wondered,' he said. 'For the last six months I've been telling myself I hoped you'd find someone who wouldn't hurt you. But when I saw you again I knew how bloody stupid that idea was. You are mine, and I might find it difficult not to kill any man who tried to take you away from me.'

Blair wasn't ready to face this sort of discussion; she felt weak and tired, and there was an ominous tightening in her throat. Changing the subject, she asked huskily, 'Why did you send Rilla across? Guilt?'

'No! You're good, you've got talent, possibly more than talent. You deserve your chance. You once said something about trying to live down your years as a decorator, and I knew Rilla would be the ideal person to take you in hand. She doesn't give a damn about all the old shibboleths. She's convinced you're going to write your name in the history books, and make her a fortune while you're doing it. And she is *not* my lover. She happens to be the cousin of a cousin, so she's family!'

Blair couldn't prevent the startled glance she gave him, flushing at his mirthless smile. How well he understood her!

Subdued, she muttered, 'That's all very well, but——'

'Just listen, Blair. You've made it damned clear what you thought, and it was rubbish. I showed Rilla the paintings I bought from you and she was hooked; she couldn't get up there fast enough.' He smiled sardonically. 'Now that we've got that out of the way, I'd like to tell you about my marriage.'

Blair bit her lip, unable to stop herself from flinching away from him.

'Stay there,' he said evenly, stopping her instinctive withdrawal by enfolding her hand in his and pulling it across to hold over his heart. Blair wondered erratically how the warmth of his grip could freeze her into submission. 'I need you beside me.'

Need was a strange word. She hadn't thought he *needed* a woman in anything but the most obvious physical way. A dull curiosity persuaded her to listen.

He didn't start immediately, but lay, still on his back, staring at the ceiling. Beneath her palm his heart beat in a steady rhythm. Hesitantly, choosing his words with care, he began, 'I know the last thing you want to hear about is my marriage, and to be brutally honest I don't want to discuss it, but it might help you to understand why I behaved the way I did. It's difficult, because I don't want to be disloyal to Gina.'

Blair's brows shot up. 'And being unfaithful to her isn't?' she asked acidly, yanking the sheet up with her free hand to hide her nakedness. 'My ex-husband was unfaithful to me, and I certainly considered it disloyal of him.' She tried to jerk her other hand away, but his tightened unmercifully around it until she stopped struggling and let it lie quiescent.

'Gina was bedridden.' His voice was flat and toneless, but she didn't make the mistake of thinking there was no emotion behind the three words.

Blair's face went white. 'What?'

'Yes. She had a stroke six years ago, the week before we were to have been married. It was an appalling tragedy. She was only twenty-seven. At first her doctors—well, we all hoped that she would regain full use of her faculties, but she was convinced that to do that she needed to be married to me, so—we went ahead with the wedding.'

'Only it didn't work.' Blair felt sick, racked by pain at the unfairness of life.

'No.' He was very still, but she could hear the heavy thudding of his heart. In the same flat monotone he said, 'She was angry and despairing, of course, when she realised that she was never going to get better. There was nothing I could do for her but try to make her happy. That didn't work either. There was no prospect of a normal life, of children, but I couldn't divorce her; she relied completely on me. Besides,' his voice was sharp with sarcasm, 'I owed her my loyalty.'

'I'm so sorry.' Poor Hugh, she thought, seeing at last the hell his sense of responsibility had led him into.

But he should have told her. He had deliberately lied to her, in fact if not in practice. Blair bit her lip until it hurt. Oh, why not admit it? It was useless trying to keep her indignation and pain whipped up to white heat; now that she knew the circumstances she could understand his behaviour.

However, understanding wasn't condoning. 'Why didn't you tell me?' she asked, tacitly admitting that she might have surrendered if he had.

'Until I met you I was absolutely faithful.' He sounded so cold, so remote that each word chilled her to the bone. 'And then—it was like a dream; you were warm and vital and you laughed—for a while I think I wanted your laughter as much as I wanted you. When we made love

I knew that I had found something beyond compare, and that you were a danger I had to leave.'

He was silent, obviously trying to muster his thoughts. Blair's breath came silently through her lips. It was obvious that this kind of revelation was painful to him; she understood why now. After years of repressing his emotions, it must be difficult to haul them out into the light of day and reveal them.

When he spoke again it was slowly, almost harshly. 'But I couldn't stay away. Finding out whether you were pregnant was only an excuse, of course, as you realised. Do I sound conceited if I say I didn't really expect you to turn me away? My need for you was so great I thought you must feel the same way.'

'I did,' she confessed. 'That's why I was so intransigent. Like you, I was afraid.'

He laughed soundlessly, mirthlessly. 'You certainly didn't seem afraid. You were magnificent, like a Valkyrie. I was confused, and angry, and desperate, but one thing I understood. I'd hurt you, and I didn't ever want to hurt you again. That altered all the rules. I wanted to tell you about Gina, to explain—although at that stage I didn't realise I loved you; I still thought it was just desire, and the need for a kind of companionship I'd never experienced with a woman before. Then at the Chapmans' I overheard you being fairly scathing about loyalty. What you said made it too damned plain that if I told you I had a wife you'd show me the door. And I couldn't do it. I needed you too much.'

Again that word. *Needed . . .*

'Yes, I remember.' Blair pushed her free hand through her hair, sweeping it back from her cheek. 'I suppose I have a thing about it. The man I was engaged to when I was twenty-two said he loved me, but he couldn't be faithful. And Gerald, my ex-husband, left me for a girl he'd been having an affair with for several months.'

'I see.' He was silent for a while, finally saying slowly, 'That explains a lot. I knew you wanted me, but you were happy in your life, you were a mature, confident, successful woman, the antithesis of poor Gina. You could have had any man you wanted. And you had ethics, high standards. Would you have sent me away, Blair?'

She bit her lip. 'I don't know,' she said in a troubled voice, unable to lie, yet not able to discern the truth. 'Perhaps, although if you'd told me about your marriage—why you couldn't leave her... It was not telling me that made me so furious—I thought, God, another man's done it to you, lied to you and fooled you... I don't know. I just don't know.'

'It doesn't matter. I decided quite cold-bloodedly not to tell you. I told myself I'd take what I could get from you and pay for it later. You didn't seem interested in marriage, and yes, I suppose I was guilty of stereotyping you as the arty bohemian. You have a way of looking at a man that makes him think of all sorts of hidden, decadent delights.' He turned his head to look at her. 'I was deceiving myself, of course, trying to find a reason for making you my mistress, because I knew that I couldn't afford to fall in love with you.'

Her hiss of indrawn breath must have warned him for he said urgently, 'Listen, please, and then you can say what you want to. So I decided that eventually, when you really trusted me, I'd tell you about my marriage. I suppose I just hoped for the best.' In a very dry voice he finished, 'It's not characteristic, believe me. I despise people who depend on luck. I suppose it was ironically appropriate that unfaithfulness was the one thing you couldn't forgive.'

'What made me so furious—still makes me furious—is that when I found out about your wife I felt you'd been unfaithful to *me*.'

He suddenly rolled over on to his side, his eyes gleaming with unrestrained triumph. 'So you love me.'

'Of course I love you,' she said, and to her horror the tears filled her eyes.

'Darling.' He was shaken, his face white. 'My heart, my golden summer girl, please don't cry.'

He gathered her up in his arms, stroking the long, lovely line of her back while she wept, murmuring love words and words of regret until she stopped crying and just lay bonelessly against him, held in the comforting strength of his arms, dazed by enchantment. For the first time ever in her life she felt protected, completely secure.

It was perilously, dangerously seductive to lie like that, sensuality in abeyance for the moment, cradled as though she was the most precious thing in his universe.

'I'm sorry,' he said into her hair. 'God, the last thing I want to do is hurt you, yet I've done it so often! I'd given up any thoughts of love, of leading a normal life, and then—I saw you and I went mad, I think. I was greedy, so I grabbed, without thinking of anything beyond my own needs, and hurt you even more than your wretched husband did. Tell me about him. How in the name of God could he be unfaithful to you?' His voice held a complex mixture of wonder and jealousy.

Blair sighed. 'He thought he had a good reason for being unfaithful. A year before he left me I'd been in El Amir when the present Emir took over. Do you remember?'

His arms tightened. 'Yes, I remember. Foreigners were interned for a while, weren't they? Don't tell me your husband found another woman when you were over there?'

'No. Not then. We were rounded up and taken into the mountains—for our protection, they said, and I think it probably was. Unfortunately for me our gaoler, who was the local chieftain, took a shine to me; he decided I'd make a rather nice addition to his harem. I objected, of course, but he ignored that. After all, I'd have a definite position in his household; I wouldn't be a wife, but I wouldn't be just a concubine, either. Everyone knows that women in the West have been totally unfeminised by their upbringing, so he sent in a couple of women to teach me all about sex, El Amir style.'

Hugh swore, luridly and swiftly, the blunt words emphasised by the softness of his voice. Blair felt every muscle in his body harden into an iron stasis, felt the effort of will it took for him to relax. His gentle touch on her cheek was the antithesis of the savage darkness in his hooded eyes. 'Did he rape you?'

'No, he didn't have time. Kieran Sinclair called in contacts and came galloping over the border on an Arabian horse to rescue me.' She smiled, but it was a poor, wobbly effort. 'I'd been so afraid for so long, shut up and alone, treated as though the only value I had for anyone was my sexuality—not even that, just my body—that when I got back the whole idea of sex turned me off totally. I couldn't let Gerald near me, and so—he strayed. Thereby,' she said with an ironic little smile, 'proving that the only part of me that was of any value to him, too, was my body.'

He frowned. 'But you were so responsive with me——'

'Yes, well, the therapist told me that I'd get over it; I just needed time.' Flushing, she looked away.

'And everything I did must have convinced you that I was just like the others—I wanted only that beautiful, maddeningly desirable body too. I told you I loved you, and then you discovered that I had a wife, so brutally.' His voice was quiet, thoughtful, his expression sombre, a nerve flicking in his jaw. 'After Gina's death I hated myself, wallowed in guilt and pain, because I was glad Gina was dead, and I felt as though my happiness had killed her. I had to come back to you, but when you told me to get the hell out of your life it seemed that I was being justly punished.'

'I see.' And at last she did. The cold rejection that had hurt her so much had been merely his way of dealing with his turbulent, painful emotions.

'I went through hell, but in some obscure way I thought I deserved it. I'd betrayed you both. I even wanted to push you away, to blame you, so that I could punish myself.'

'Then why did you arrange all this?'

His smile was self-derisory. 'Because I came to my senses. I should never have married Gina, but I thought I owed it to her. And I loved her, in a way.'

'You must have loved her very much. Most men would never have dreamed of marrying her.'

'What I felt for her was affection and lust; I decided that as I hadn't ever fallen headlong in love it clearly wasn't going to happen to me, so I might as well marry someone I liked, someone who was good in bed, who'd make an excellent mother for my children.'

'Cold-blooded.' She couldn't hide the stinging snap in the word.

'I am cold-blooded,' he said quietly. 'It's only with you that I lose control. I married her because I thought she needed me, and because I owed her my loyalty. When she died I think I went a little insane for a while. It seemed so unfair that her life should have ended like that. I had to grieve for her. It took me months to work through the implications, but as soon as I'd accepted that the time I snatched with you meant more to me than all the rest of my life put together I knew I wasn't going to rest until I'd got you back.'

'Then why didn't you just come back? Why the elaborate charade with Rilla and the gallery?'

Her disillusion must have shown in her voice because he said sternly, 'It's no charade. Rilla is thrilled to have you join her. I wanted you to have your success. You didn't have a hope of getting away, Blair. I want you rather more than I want to breathe, and I had my sights set on you. I was prepared to stalk you for years if it was necessary, do whatever I had to do to get you back. I accepted that I'd probably killed your love, but I knew you wanted me. I decided I'd work on that, make you admit it, and build from there.'

'Arrogant swine,' she said without heat.

His sapphire glance was brilliant with amusement and tenderness. 'Yes, I'm afraid so. But I'm an ordinary man, Blair, just a man so in love for the first time in his life that he can't think straight.'

An ordinary man? Blair almost laughed out loud at the sheer absurdity of such a statement. Hugh was a man with a particularly rigid sense of responsibility, and the strength of character to marry a woman who needed him and try to make the best of it, even though it meant giving up his dreams of a normal life to do it. No, he was no ordinary man, he was the man for her, now and for the rest of her life.

Blinking, she tried to speak, but her mouth trembled and she didn't know what to say, how to tell him. However, he seemed to know, for he pulled her across him in one smooth movement.

'Don't cry any more,' he said, the stringent control gone from his mouth, his expression, his eyes. He was looking at her with passion and desire and need, openly, nakedly offering himself. 'I love you. I'll love you until I die, and beyond. Is there the remotest chance that you can forgive me?'

'Oh, Hugh, you fool,' she whispered. 'Of course I forgive you. I've loved you from the minute I looked across that room and saw you talking to Sam. Why on earth do you think I made love with you so soon?'

He laughed softly, triumphantly, and his face lit up with the unalloyed joy of a lover. 'When can we get married, then?'

'As soon as you want to,' she said promptly.

'Where would you like to live?'

'Wherever you are.'

He laughed. Then they both froze. Someone called out from below, 'Blair? Where are you?'

To the sound of Tegan's footsteps coming too quickly up the stairs Hugh dragged the sheet over them both. Embarrassment curdled Blair's blood. She risked a look at Hugh's face and saw him start to laugh deeply, with the satisfaction of a man whose life had suddenly come together.

'Blair, what on earth——' Tegan's voice was horrified as she stopped in the doorway.

Blair hid her face in Hugh's shoulder, unable to meet Tegan's eyes. She could feel the movement in his chest as he laughed.

There followed what could only be described as a pregnant pause. Then, 'Hello,' Tegan said cheerfully. 'You must be Hugh Bannatyne. It's about time you turned up. Kieran was saying last night that he thought he might have to go looking for you. Welcome to the family. Next time, why don't you knock instead of breaking through the door? And would you please call Kieran, because I think this baby is on its way?'

Ten hours later Blair was holding her godson with awe-struck hands, her eyes so worshipful that everyone else in the room blinked. 'He's beautiful,' she sighed. 'Oh, Tegan, he's just wonderful.' She beamed around, her customary indolence swallowed up by happiness. Her eyes skidded to a halt on Hugh's face. 'I think we should have one,' she said firmly.

He grinned. 'All right.'

Tegan looked wistful. 'Don't you dare get married before I get my waist back.'

They all laughed, and Hugh said, 'How long will that take? Because I warn you I'm not waiting more than a week.'

Blair's eyes widened. 'A week?'

'That's it.'

'But my parents are roaming along the Silk Road!'

'Tough,' he said ruthlessly. 'Give that baby back to its father, and come out into the corridor where we can discuss things without disturbing mother or child.'

'Blair,' Tegan said, smiling at her husband, 'just give in. When a man looks like that he's going to get his own way.'

Blair dropped a kiss on to her godson's downy head, said, 'Hold him carefully,' and handed him back to Kieran, watching him anxiously as he tucked his son into his arms as skilfully as though he had half a dozen other children. He looked down at his son, and then at his wife, with something Blair had never seen in his expression before. Swallowing, she went out of the room with Hugh, leaving behind three people who couldn't have been happier.

'A week,' Hugh said sternly.

'All right.'

He laughed, and in front of the interested gaze of two nurses and a large green teddy bear propped in a chair kissed her with a slow, enjoyable determination. 'I don't suppose you'll be as amenable as this very often, but I'm enjoying it. Welcome to the future, my dearest love.'

Misty-eyed, Blair smiled. All her dreams were coming true. In place of the paradise she thought she had lost she had this Eden, fresh and new and beautiful, their own private paradise regained.

INDULGE A LITTLE 6947 SWEEPSTAKES
NO PURCHASE NECESSARY

HERE'S HOW THE SWEEPSTAKES WORKS:
The Harlequin Reader Service shipments for January, February and March 1994 will contain, respectively, coupons for entry into three prize drawings: a trip for two to San Francisco, an Alaskan cruise for two and a trip for two to Hawaii. To be eligible for any drawing using an Entry Coupon, simply complete and mail according to directions.

There is no obligation to continue as a Reader Service subscriber to enter and be eligible for any prize drawing. You may also enter any drawing by hand printing your name and address on a 3" x 5" card and the destination of the prize you wish that entry to be considered for (i.e., San Francisco trip, Alaskan cruise or Hawaiian trip). Send your 3" x 5" entries to: Indulge a Little 6947 Sweepstakes, c/o Prize Destination you wish that entry to be considered for, P.O. Box 1315, Buffalo, NY 14269-1315, U.S.A. or Indulge a Little 6947 Sweepstakes, P.O. Box 610, Fort Erie, Ontario L2A 5X3, Canada.

To be eligible for the San Francisco trip, entries must be received by 4/30/94; for the Alaskan cruise, 5/31/94; and the Hawaiian trip, 6/30/94. No responsibility is assumed for lost, late or misdirected mail. Sweepstakes open to residents of the U.S. (except Puerto Rico) and Canada, 18 years of age or older. All applicable laws and regulations apply. Sweepstakes void wherever prohibited.

For a copy of the Official Rules, send a self-addressed, stamped envelope (WA residents need not affix return postage) to: Indulge a Little 6947 Rules, P.O. Box 4631, Blair, NE 68009, U.S.A.

INDR93

INDULGE A LITTLE 6947 SWEEPSTAKES
NO PURCHASE NECESSARY

HERE'S HOW THE SWEEPSTAKES WORKS:
The Harlequin Reader Service shipments for January, February and March 1994 will contain, respectively, coupons for entry into three prize drawings: a trip for two to San Francisco, an Alaskan cruise for two and a trip for two to Hawaii. To be eligible for any drawing using an Entry Coupon, simply complete and mail according to directions.

There is no obligation to continue as a Reader Service subscriber to enter and be eligible for any prize drawing. You may also enter any drawing by hand printing your name and address on a 3" x 5" card and the destination of the prize you wish that entry to be considered for (i.e., San Francisco trip, Alaskan cruise or Hawaiian trip). Send your 3" x 5" entries to: Indulge a Little 6947 Sweepstakes, c/o Prize Destination you wish that entry to be considered for, P.O. Box 1315, Buffalo, NY 14269-1315, U.S.A. or Indulge a Little 6947 Sweepstakes, P.O. Box 610, Fort Erie, Ontario L2A 5X3, Canada.

To be eligible for the San Francisco trip, entries must be received by 4/30/94; for the Alaskan cruise, 5/31/94; and the Hawaiian trip, 6/30/94. No responsibility is assumed for lost, late or misdirected mail. Sweepstakes open to residents of the U.S. (except Puerto Rico) and Canada, 18 years of age or older. All applicable laws and regulations apply. Sweepstakes void wherever prohibited.

For a copy of the Official Rules, send a self-addressed, stamped envelope (WA residents need not affix return postage) to: Indulge a Little 6947 Rules, P.O. Box 4631, Blair, NE 68009, U.S.A.

INDR93

INDULGE A LITTLE
SWEEPSTAKES

OFFICIAL ENTRY COUPON

This entry must be received by: JUNE 30, 1994
This month's winner will be notified by: JULY 15, 1994
Trip must be taken between: AUGUST 31, 1994-AUGUST 31, 1995

YES, I want to win the 3-Island Hawaiian vacation for two. I understand that the prize includes round-trip airfare, first-class hotels and pocket money as revealed on the "wallet" scratch-off card.

Name________________________________

Address ____________________ Apt. ________

City________________________________

State/Prov.______________ Zip/Postal Code__________

Daytime phone number_________________________
(Area Code)

Account #_____________________________

Return entries with invoice in envelope provided. Each book in this shipment has two entry coupons—and the more coupons you enter, the better your chances of winning!

© 1993 HARLEQUIN ENTERPRISES LTD. MONTH3